Take a Leaf Out of My Book

and other stories

Ann Burnett

To Annie,

Merry Christmas,

Love from Postman Pat

X

Published by Ladybug Publications

ISBN 978 0 9558540 1 9

Cover design: © Brian Craig at TALL: art design photograph

These stories are works of fiction. They've all won prizes in various competitions but they've never been published until now.

Contents

Take a Leaf Out of My Book

'Take a leaf out of my book,' he says, spittle frothing at the side of his frog mouth, his eyes popping out like marbles. 'Work hard like me and you'll be rich too.'

I can work as hard as I can but I will never be rich, not with what he pays me. Enough for my phone and quick calls home to my mother and a little left over each week. No, I will never be rich working for him.

He has a shop, a cheap, sells everything shop, and a stall in the market. He lives in this large house with more rooms than he can use, drives a Mercedes and a Porsche and has a Chanel-scented wife who spends more in one shopping trip than I earn in a year. I tidy her clothes and shoes in the huge walk-in wardrobe and sometimes I try on her Jimmy Choos to see how they feel.

But shoes and clothes don't make her happy. The couple argue. They have no children and he blames her. He suggests she see an exorcist, a shaman, she should go back to her home village and sacrifice a goat; she says he should be tested in the fertility clinic. He does not like this. He shouts and throws his glass against the wall, red wine spattering on to the carpet. So she goes out and buys more clothes, more shoes, more comfort while I clear up the debris and scrub at the red stains.

He has friends, 'business associates' as he calls them, over for dinner and as I serve spiced chicken and dried fish, plantain chips and peanut stew, he tells them that those who use banks are fools.

'Lets the taxman see how rich they are. Lets the taxman take his cut. No, I keep my money elsewhere.' He taps the side of his nose while chewing noisily on his food. He takes in money every day at his shop and market stall, hands a wad to his wife and stuffs the rest in his pockets. They bulge with money.

I smell his rank sweat as I fill his plate with more rice and stew. He eats too much, too fast. Elegant, he is not. Mannerly, he is not. A good employer? I think not.

'Take a leaf out of my book,' he says as I dust the shelves in the room he calls his library. 'I am from a small village like you. I came here with nothing. Now I am a very rich man. You too, can be like me.'

I have no intention of being like him.

On days when I have some time to myself, I walk out of the house and along the street to the shops. The sun never seems to shine here and the sky is low with clouds. I miss the clear blue skies of my home, the hot sun on my back, the heavy scent of the cattle. This country always feels cold to me and I shiver in my thin African clothes. I pass a girl begging at the foot of the church steps. She looks as cold as me, sitting there on the concrete, her hand holding out a polystyrene coffee cup in the hope of some change.

I like it when I reach the shops. I go into the big department store and stand for a moment in the doorway letting the blast of warm air flow down over me. I spend as long as I can in the store, moving from department to department, up and down the escalators. There is one part I love to visit, the ladies' coats department. I have seen the coat I crave, the coat I would buy if I were as rich as him. It is a soft dove-grey, padded like a quilt and with a hood trimmed in matching fur. I try it on one day, shrugging off my thin jacket and slipping my arms through the silk-lined sleeves. I wrap myself in it, pulling the hood over my head and feel for the first time, warm and... what is the word? Snug. Yes, snug.

The sales assistant admires me in it but I glance at the price tag and regretfully hand the coat back to her. But I dream of that coat all the way back home. No, not home. Back to the house where I live – and work.

On Fridays, his wife insists he comes to prayers with her. Afterwards, he shuts himself in his library and must not be disturbed. I don't know what he does there. He doesn't read the books. He must have bought them in bulk to fill his shelves. Some have reduced stickers on them. They are all unread, hardbacks neatly arranged by size and colour on the shelves. Homer's *Iliad* is next to Martina Cole is next to *Jane Eyre* is next to... whatever title matches it in height apparently. There is a complete set of Encyclopaedia Britannica along one shelf, dark red leather bindings etched with gold lettering. AU-BE, ST-TA, LI-MO. Even they are out of sequence.

I slide the feather duster along the tops of the books and yearn to read them. He does not realise the wealth that many of them contain: imagination, escapism, learning, knowledge. None of these is he interested in. He only wants money for what it can buy him. But he would notice if I took a book down to read. There would be a gap and even if I only read on Fridays, I would bend the spines, ruffle the pages, meddle with their perfection.

I shouldn't complain about him. Many maids are worse off than me. He doesn't beat me, he doesn't molest me - his wife is too quick and knowing for that - and I do get paid a little. I should be grateful.

He brought me here under false pretences. A promise of a home, an education in return for some domestic duties. A chance for me to better myself, to earn enough to support my family.

'I am giving you an education,' he yells at me when I ask if I can go to school to study for exams. 'I am teaching you. Follow my example and you will learn everything you need to know. Take a leaf out of my book.'

I decide to do as he says. I will take a leaf out of his book. Every one of his books. I will cut out one page from each of them and throw it away. He will never notice as he does not read them but I will know.

I find a letter opener, sharp, shaped like a dagger. It will slice down a page very smoothly. It seems like sacrilege to me, to damage a book in this way but I am only doing what he told me.

On Friday I wait till they leave for prayers. Then I slip into the library. I start with the first book on the top shelf and open it. It is *Things Fall Apart* by Chinua Achebe. Our most famous writer. I wonder if he has ever heard of him. Tentatively I lift it down and open it at a random page. There is a £20 note tucked into the fold. I turn to another page. £10 this time. Notes hide between the pages.

I take the paper knife and draw it down the inside of a page. It falls out leaving almost no sign of the cut. I take some of the notes too. Next I lift down Charles Dickens' *Great Expectations*. It lives up to its title. I do the same to each book along the shelf, carefully replacing them in the same random order and making sure he cannot tell that they have been disturbed.

The pages I tear into tiny pieces and toss them into a waste bin on my way to a nearby bank. I show my passport, open an account and pay in the money. I do this every week and he does not notice. I am not stealing. I am only doing as he instructed.

Today, though, is different. I take my passport and first I go to the bank. Then I visit the travel agent next door where I buy my plane ticket. I leave for home tonight.

I have one more thing to do.

I have money left over from buying my ticket so I walk to the department store past the girl begging on the church steps. It is beginning to rain again, a cold, drenching rain that seeps through my clothing and chills me to the bone. The girl pulls a thin, grey blanket around herself; her hands are blue, her fingernails rimmed with dirt. She looks ill, uncared for. She hangs her head; she does not look at me as I pass by, merely holds out her cup in desperate hope.

In the store, I rush up the escalators to the ladies' coats. What if it has been sold? What if there are none left in my size? But it is still hanging there, the lustrous grey coat with the silvery fur around the hood. I slip off my wet jacket and try it on once again. It is everything I want it to be, snug and warm, sheltering me from this bitter cold. I look at the price tag and this time, when the assistant approaches, I say, 'I'll take it.'

I fly out of the store clutching the bag with the coat inside. As I near the church, I see the girl stand up and empty the cup of the few coins she has collected. She stuffs them in the pocket of her jeans and gathers up the wad of newspaper she has been sitting on. She is about to leave.

'Wait!' I call, rushing up. 'Here, this is for you. Take it. It will keep you warm and dry.' I tug the coat out of the bag and hand it to her.

I help her slip her arms through the sleeves and wrap the coat around her skinny frame. She sighs as she pulls the hood over her head and smiles. Her eyes crinkle up with pleasure.

'For me?'

I nod and walk on quickly without looking back. I am going to the airport. I am going home. Really home.

I have taken a leaf out of his book. I have done what he told me. I have learned much. But I will never be like him.

Are You Listening?

Susan switched on the radio which sat on the window ledge in the kitchen. It was slightly greasy to the touch, its smooth surfaces impregnated with several years of cooking while the speaker meshes were coated with dust in their hard-to-clean crevices. Today she wanted to listen to Woman's Hour while she tackled the kitchen floor. Jenni Murray's soothing voice rippled through the kitchen as she first swept the cat hairs, crumbs and assorted debris into a pile in the middle of the floor.

It was Monday and she was feeling good. As she glanced out of the kitchen window, she spotted a large black bird searching for crumbs from the bird feeders she hung on the apple tree, now laden with its crop of fruit. The bird was large for a crow, she thought, and its beak was heavy duty. A raven perhaps?

Susan gathered up the sweepings in the dustpan and emptied it into the pedal bin which she kept out of the way in the utility room. A piece of paper had stuck to the pan and by the time she removed it, put the brush and pan away and took out the mop ready for her next task, the voice on the radio had changed.

Are you listening? Carefully?

You'll not be sitting comfortably, though. I know you'll be doing something else as you hear my voice. Perhaps you're busy in the kitchen cleaning the sink or cooking or at work in the office or having a break. Wherever you are, I'm here too.

And you'll be listening to me.

Carefully.

Susan filled the bucket with warm water and added some washing up liquid. The suds foamed as she listened. Was it time for the Woman's Hour Drama already? She glanced at the clock on the oven. No, it was only twenty past ten. So what topic was this? The voice was neither male or female, quite deep though not warm like Jenni Murray's. Was it a man or a woman? She dunked the mop in the bucket, squeezed it out and swished it across the floor. A wet shine exposed the parts she'd washed.

There's nothing to be scared of. After all, it's daylight and you're safe at home or at work or in the office. Nothing's going to happen.

The mop clunked against a chair leg as she pushed it under the small wooden table used for their breakfasts and morning coffees. It must be some author giving a reading from their latest book, she thought. A momentary crossness flitted over her face. She would have liked to have known what book it was; she could have downloaded it on to her kindle. Now that she could concentrate enough to read, she was partial to a bit of horror or murder mystery, something to make her cower under the bedclothes after she switched off the light. Not perhaps the best subject for her but certainly a genre she enjoyed.

Those little noises that are going on around you are nothing to be frightened of. Nothing at all. They're just ordinary, everyday noises.

Aren't they?

The fridge clicked on and hummed quietly to itself, the thermostat keeping the milk, orange juice and tonight's lamb chops at the necessary temperature. She was looking forward to cooking the meat. She'd serve them with some mash and frozen peas. They both liked that.

Susan bent to sweep the mop further under the table. If she was being thorough she supposed she ought to move the table out of the way but today she couldn't be bothered, anyway she wanted to hear the rest of the extract and maybe Jenni would give the name of the book.

So when you hear talk of witches and ghosts and broomsticks and evil spirits, you won't be frightened, will you? They don't exist. They're all in the mind. Black cats can cross your path and rub against your legs and the hair on the back of your neck will nevermore begin to rise.

So that's what it was, a Hallowe'en ghost story. Probably not a book at all. She rinsed the mop in the bucket again and wrung it out in the perforated cup at the top. Pity, it sounded quite good. It would make a good book. She poked the mop into the edges of the vinyl along the skirting board. A small black spider sprinted along ahead of her. She didn't mind. She'd let it go. Susan wasn't one of those women who couldn't bear the sight of spiders. Actually, she quite liked them. Their webs were so beautifully made that sometimes she left them hanging from the cornices like spindrift instead of dusting them away. The spider crept through a minute space and disappeared.

Upstairs, the shower head spat out a dribble of water left over from her morning shower. The sound didn't penetrate her consciousness, it happened every morning, just one of the familiar sounds of home.

And those odd little noises that you hear don't cause your heart to beat more loudly or you to pause in whatever it is you are doing. They're nothing to be afraid of. They're just ordinary, everyday noises.

Susan laughed out loud. 'Are you talking to me?' she said to the radio, swinging the mop round in a final sweep.

9

So when you hear....

The sound of slow footsteps emanated from the radio.

....you know they're just the footsteps of somebody in the next room or upstairs, don't you? And you're not alone are you?

'Yes, I'm alone,' said Susan. She lifted the bucket of dirty water up to the sink and poured it down the drain. It gurgled and sloshed about, drowning out the radio though it almost seemed to Susan that the broadcast paused till it was quiet again.

It's all in the mind, all that nonsense about ghosts and witches and things that go bump because they only go bump in the night, don't they? And it's not night-time, is it? It's still daylight. You can still see outside into the garden so there's absolutely nothing to be scared of.

Is there?

She stared out of the window, still holding the bucket against the sink. It was uncanny how that story was mimicking life, her life. It was certainly well-written, almost as if the author had been standing behind her, looking over her shoulder as she wrote. As Susan continued to stare, the big black bird in the garden turned its head to look at her. She shuddered.

This wasn't getting her anywhere. She marched the bucket and mop into the utility room and set them to dry. She'd better get started on the soup. A pile of vegetables sat unused in the fridge and as it was frozen peas that night, she thought she'd make soup to use them up. And she enjoyed listening to Woman's Hour while she worked.

She took out some onions, a bag of carrots and a wrinkled parsnip. Waste not, want not, she heard her mother's voice say from the past. She had just taken the knife to an onion when she paused. Had the radio gone off or had she switched it off?

10

Then the voice spoke again.

Why have you stopped doing your work? You are listening, I know, but you can still carry on. Are you listening for something else? Or are you thinking about what I've just said? You're not beginning to feel scared are you?

Goose bumps rippled up Susan's arm. What an extraordinary story. And long too. Was this guy taking over the whole of Woman's Hour? She fiddled with the radio's buttons, checking that she had the correct preset station. Hisses and white noise came from the other stations but Radio 4 was loud and clear.

You don't believe all those stories about souls wandering for evermore without rest or vampires cursed to seek out the night and their helpless victims? Anyway, it's daylight just now. What is there to be scared of? There are no owls hooting or gusts of wind rattling window panes, are there?

So why are you scared? Because you are, aren't you?

Susan chopped furiously at the onion. Bits of it flew off the chopping board as she worked. This was getting ridiculous. Where was Jenni Murray? She stabbed at the buttons again in an attempt to find a different station. Some nice soothing Classic FM would be better than this. Had she taken her meds today? She couldn't remember. Frantically she mentally went through the morning. Mark got up, brought her a cup of tea, yes, yes she had taken them. The tea had been too hot at first, she remembered.

In another room, something fell with a dull thud.

Did you hear that? Are you wondering what it was? Why are you looking around? Do you think there's somebody else about?

You would hear them, wouldn't you?

11

Susan thumped down the off switch. She could feel her heartbeat in the back of her throat and her hands shivered around the knife. The onion lay on the chopping board, cut not into her usual diced pieces but slaughtered and dismembered. She picked up a carrot and made herself top and tail it and scrape off a layer of skin. Her breathing was harsh and quicker than usual. Breathe slowly, she told herself. You're hyperventilating. Take your time. Concentrate on chopping the carrot. You're making soup. You're at home. All is well. It's only the radio. It's not in your head. It's not in your head.

She made herself slice the carrot into precise, regular chunks before tossing them into the pot and starting on the next one. She continued at her task, letting her neck and shoulders ease down, her back unwind and slouch forward, her heartbeat slow to a normal rhythm. Good. The relaxation classes had been worth it. She could control her intrusive thoughts.

The radio hissed quietly. She thought she could hear the speaker's breath in the background.

A slight cough sounded almost directly behind her, it seemed.

You would know if someone was close by, wouldn't you?

Susan straightened, her hand tightening around the vegetable knife, all senses on alert. Slowly, so slowly, she made herself turn. No-one was there. The house was silent. Outside a car passed along the road. Her body slumped. 'Damned radio,' she said aloud. Her voice sounded almost normal in the silence. She blew a stray hair from her forehead and threw the knife down on the chopping board. She wiped her sweaty hands down the side of her jeans and forced out a laugh. 'Damned radio! It's not me, it's the radio.'

She pressed the on/off switch again, checking that this time she had switched it off. Weird, she thought. It's not like

12

Woman's Hour to carry something like that. I wonder what they're playing at.

Susan leant on the kitchen unit until she stopped shaking and her pulse slowed. 'You've an overactive imagination,' she scolded. 'Get on with the soup, for goodness sake. You're fine. You're not having another breakdown, you're fine.'

She picked up the last carrot and chopped the top off it just as she heard the first heavy, slow footstep.

And if they were coming near you, you would hear them, wouldn't you? You wouldn't be frightened because what is there to be frightened of, except what's going on inside your own head? What are you thinking about?

Susan dropped the knife and fled to the lounge. She flung herself on to the sofa and reached for her phone. She would phone the police, her husband, anyone and say......what?

Are you sitting comfortably now?

I hope so.

Goodbye.

Susan heard a door shut and footsteps retreating. In the kitchen, Jenni Murray chattered quietly to her unseen audience while outside the big black bird flapped its wings and flew off.

Dougan's Last Case

Tuesday 12.30am. Outside Preston Street again. Third time this week. The light in the upstairs room comes on. I try to stretch my legs between the brake pedal and the clutch to bring the circulation back.

12.36am. The front door opens and my quarry emerges. He walks to his car, buttoning up his black fleece with the football club logo on the left chest, unlocks the door and gets in. The engine takes three turns to start this time. I wonder again why he doesn't get it serviced. I could give him the name of the wee man I take my Golf to. I start it up and pull out discreetly after the silver Jag, letting another car get between us. It doesn't matter. I know where he's heading. Back to Troon and his missus with no doubt, another tale about being held up at the office. He visits Sophie Good about twice a week, three times if he can work it, and she charges him £50 a time for her services, with emphasis on the second syllable. I know because I asked her. She charged me £100 for that information and I didn't get any extras either. It will come under the heading of expenses on my bill.

1.16am. He turns into the driveway of his house. He's put his foot down all the way along the M77. The Golf kept up, just. If he hadn't stopped for a leak at the side of the motorway, I'd have lost him. I wonder how many more instances of his infidelity I need to show to his missus before she's satisfied with the evidence. I've been tagging him for nearly a month now and he's visited Sophie G. nine times, picked up another prostitute at Anderston Cross, been drunk out of his skull twice and had four fish suppers with a pickled onion. You can't say I'm not thorough. Trusty, Thorough and True. That's the motto of my firm. James Dougan, Private Investigators Inc. Trusty, Thorough and True. The (ex) wife said it sounded like a firm of dodgy lawyers. There's only me but I like to give the impression of a larger enterprise, hence the plural 'investigators'. I log his return home in my dictaphone and head back home myself.

8.36am. The phone jars me awake. I shake my head to get rid of the sleep, sit up straight and press answer. 'Private Investigators Inc. James Dougan speaking. How (here I lower my voice to a comforting burr) may I be of service to you?'

'I need youse to come right away,' a female voice answers. Newton Mearns with undertones of Possil. 'Like now. Can youse?'

'Where to? And why?' Saltcoats with a touch of the Taggarts and a soupçon of Jimmy Cagney.

She gives the address. Miles away, of course. I'll have to look it up on the street map, my Golf not being a model with sat nav.

'And you are?'

'Chanelle Connolly.' Big Brother meets the Big Yin.

'I'll be there.'

10.25am. At last I pull up outside the house. The street map was a bit vague, there being nothing there according to it. And I see why. It's the only house in a cul-de sac. It's a new ranch type bungalow set inside huge ironwork gates with a CCTV

15

camera and no doubt a couple of rottweilers prowling around. I press the buzzer and wait safely inside the car.

The dogs are more bull mastiff with a touch of alsatian and I nearly run over them in their determination to bite my tyres. A skinny wee woman in black leather trousers and a frilly pink blouse shouts at them and they slink away. I check the coast is clear and get out my car. I put my fedora on and shrug my shoulders more comfortably inside my trench coat.

'Ms Connolly.'

'It's Mrs. Ah thought youse were coming right away. This is important.'

'I came as soon as I could.' I am not going to mention I got lost or that I finished my weetabix and tea before setting out. Image is all with the punters.

'Come in.'

I follow her through the hall and into what I take to be the lounge. The walls are tiger skin, the sofa is cream leather with a leopard skin throw and the bar has a padded pink leather front to it and some rather good malts behind it. Drug dealer chic. A large blue teddy bear with a tartan bow sits on one of the arm chairs. I sit on the other, placing my fedora on the coffee table beside House Beautiful, Heat and Silicon Chicks.

I lean back and fix my eyes on her black rimmed, purple lidded peepers.

'How can I help you?'

'I need you to follow Buggerlugs and find out where he's going.'

I'm no longer astonished by the names married couples give each other.

'Describe him.'

'Well, he's gingerish, short-haired, green eyes...'

'How old?' I take out my notebook to jot down the info.

16

'Does it matter?' Chanelle is chewing the side of her mouth.

'Of course.'

'Six, I think.'

I raise an eyebrow in a quizzical manner. Surely not a...? It is. At that moment, a large, fat, ginger cat pads into the room.

'Ah don't know where he's went. Ah think sumday's feeding him. An' see if it's that bunch of fenians across the road...!'

'He's an orange cat then.' But my little joke passes her by.

'Youse can see that, for god's sake. He's got diabetes. He's no supposed to eat onything except what ah gie him.' Her accent is deteriorating by the sentence. 'Charlie just dotes on him. Says he'll gie a doin tae onywan laying a finger on Buggerlugs.'

I've no doubt he means it. I decide I'd rather not be involved.

10.44am. Despite my raising my charges considerably, she still insists I take on the Case of the Mystery Cat Feeder. I do not want to spend my time chasing a drug dealers's adored moggie round houses, though for the price I've quoted her, I could clear a very tidy profit. And I need the cash. For some reason, the inhabitants of the West of Scotland do not see the need for the services of a private eye as often as I would like them to.

Wednesday 7.23am. I'm wearing a tracksuit I dug out from the back of the wardrobe and jogging on the spot to keep warm. Chanelle Connolly is about to let the cat out the back door and I will be following its progress for the rest of the morning. I can't wait.

The door opens and Buggerlugs sticks its nose out. It sees me and refuses to go any further. I sense Chanelle's foot meeting its rear end as it suddenly erupts out on to the patio. It sits down and washes said area of its anatomy.

7.28am. Ablutions complete, Buggerlugs saunters over to my trainers and sniffs. I wait. Buggerlugs sits and waits too.

7.39am. Cat gets up and strolls round to front of house. I stroll round after it. I am unable to feel my feet from the cold. Buggerlugs disappears through the hedge into the nearest neighbour's garden. I sprint to the front gates, closely followed by three barking dogs who nip my heels. Fortunately, that part of me is still frozen. I reach through the locked gates and frantically stab the buzzer. Chanelle answers.

'Yes? Who is it? Please stand in front so the camera can see youse.'

I shout. I swear. The dogs bark. The gates remain shut. I am forced to retreat to the back door, eagerly followed by Flopsy, Mopsy and Cottontail who persist in finding my trainers fascinating. Must be the smell of cat.

8.01am. Chanelle has shut the dogs in the run. I have berated her for her laxity, stupidity and thoughtlessness in letting them loose when I am investigating a serious matter. It goes over her head. I point out a frayed area at the foot of my tracksuit bottoms and say that I will add the cost of replacement designer clothing to my bill. She does not notice the New Look logo on the pocket. I insist on a drink to warm myself and to calm my nerves after such an event. She makes me tea with no sugar.

8.12am. I jog out the gates and along the street in an attempt to catch up with Buggerlugs. He (as a view of his hindquarters has revealed) could be anywhere by now. If he has any sense, he will be curled up in somebody's warm kitchen.

8.14am. By sheer luck, I spot my quarry slinking through a gate further up the street. I slink in after him and follow him round to the back garden, passing a dark blue Honda Civic in the driveway. Fortunately, the curtains are still closed in all the rooms. Buggerlugs is digging a hole for his business in a neatly tended rose bed. I stand by the back door and wait. He and I are both engrossed in this activity when suddenly my arm is grabbed and I am dragged into the kitchen and the back door slammed shut.

8.15am. I am staring into Sophie Good's red-rimmed sleepy eyes.

'What are you doing here?' she hisses.

'Mr Connolly a client of yours? Or (here I pause) are you a client of his?'

Sophie's cheeks have a red tinge which owes nothing to blusher.

'You're not going to tell them? I'm respectable here. I'm one of the folk who objected to their planning application. We don't want their sort round here. He's a nasty piece of work.'

I let a slow smile creep across my lips. 'And what exactly (another pregnant pause here) do the neighbours think your line of business is?'

She scowls. 'For your information, a care assistant at an old folk's home on permanent night duty.'

'I suppose that's half true. You take care of certain people's needs and well, none of your punters are exactly young, are they?'

'How did you find me?'

'I have my ways.' I realise my luck is changing. 'But…. (I shrug my shoulders inside my tracksuit though it's not as effective as in my trench coat. Not enough room.) …but we could come to some arrangement.' I run my hand over the worktop. Granite. And the units aren't MFI either.

'How much?'

'Two… thousand.' I wonder if I'm pushing my luck. I had meant to say hundred.

She nods. My stomach shoots butterflies in every direction.

Sophie goes out of the kitchen.

8.21am. I am clutching a bundle of old tens and twenties and making a show of counting them. 'Not that I don't trust you,' I chuckle. I thrust them into the pocket of my track suit bottoms. I see her stare at the New Look logo. I turn to leave but pause, just before I step outside.

'By the way, gonnae no feed that ginger cat. It's got diabetes. You'll kill it.'

She nods as she closes the door. Buggerlugs and I set off back to the Connolly's, my hopes fulfilled while the cat's are dashed.

8.35am. I'm getting into my car with more cash than I've had in years. Chanelle is stunned that I've solved the mystery so quickly and that it wasn't the fenians who were feeding her cat but that nice, quiet Mrs Good who thought it was a stray. She tipped me an extra £50 on top of the massive fee and expenses I've charged her.

'Ah'll mention yer name tae Charlie,' she says.
'No thanks,' I mutter.
I make a three point turn in the driveway.

8.36am. I feel a bump as I reverse. I stop and get out. A hairy, ginger lump is lying under the wheels. Oh f*§*.

Half a World Away

The first time I saw him, he was standing a little apart from the jostling, cheering crowd of men. As I looked down from the deck of the ship, I couldn't help noticing him. He alone did not shout or gesticulate to the rows of women lining the rails. Already, the men were picking out their particular fancies, pointing to them and trying to make their wishes known to the women. The men were an untidy, ill-kempt, unshaven lot, their bushy beards masking most of their faces and their battered, dirty hats shading the rest. The rickety wooden pier on which they waited led to an inn and some sheds. Beyond was nothing but swamp and mud and a well worn path leading, I presumed, to Melbourne. It was worlds away from what I had known.

My heart sank. This was where I was to spend the rest of my days. Begin a new life where no-one knew me. I had no money, no friends, no prospects. Only a bitter determination to leave England behind and forget all that had gone before. I had not expected much from my new country but this vista removed any hope I had.

The first women were clambering down the gang-plank to be surrounded by a crush of men grasping and pulling at them. It did not matter whether a woman was young or old, plain or pretty, she was immediately bombarded by offers from the waiting men. I hung back, clinging tightly to my one bag, and waited till the rest of the women disembarked and most of the men dispersed. Stumbling a little, I made my way down the gang-plank and stood at last on firm ground, the first time for many, many weeks. I swayed and, tripping over a coil of rope, went headlong. My hat flew off and my bag rolled a little way from me.

I picked myself up and directed a vicious kick at the rope.

'Ma'am.'

He was standing beside me holding my hat and my bag. To cover my embarrassment, I began to brush the dust from my skirts. He stood and watched me silently.

'Thank you,' I said, reaching out for my belongings.

'Ma'am,' he began again, still holding on to my hat and bag, 'You're from the Carlisle?'

'Yes.'

'You'll be looking for somewhere to go?'

'Yes.'

'Ma'am, I was thinking …' He stopped and looked away.

I waited.

'It's just that Melbourne is no place for a single lady like yourself.'

I smiled to myself. A lady indeed!

'You need someone to, to... take care of you. Like a husband.'

In spite of myself, I blushed.

'That's what I'm offering,' he continued in a rush. 'I'm an honest man and a hard worker. I been working the goldfields at Bendigo and I bought me a property north west of here, South Australia way. I got some money saved and together we could fix up a home and run a property. That is, if you're willing.'

I looked at him. He was taller than most men and well built. His face was covered with a heavy brown beard and shaggy brown hair hung over his forehead. His clothes were well worn and roughly patched and his hat was pulled down low over his eyes. As I looked at him, his eyes met mine. They were blue, as

23

blue as the waters in the bay and they gazed straight at me. They were honest, sincere eyes. For a moment I paused. But only a moment. What else was I to do?

'I'm willing.'

We spent our wedding night in a cheap room in one of the many hostelries in Melbourne. It was then that I saw the scars on his back.

Unthinkingly, I asked them how he came by them.

His eyes flashed.

'Don't ask me nothing. I won't ask you your past and don't you ask me mine. What's gone afore is done and best forgotten.'

I turned away. What could he know of me? I had told him nothing. But I now knew his past. I had married a convict. What was he? Thief? Rioter? Murderer?

I knelt by my bed to say my prayers. Then I climbed in beside him and blew out the candle.

We left Melbourne the next day and travelled north to Bendigo in a bullock cart loaded down with provisions and stores and with a sorry looking mule in tow. The massive animals plodded along the track mile after weary mile. I sometimes climbed down to walk ahead and enjoy the strange vista before me. The trees, thin and stringy, the shrubs a riot of exotic blooms in hectic reds and yellows.

I asked him their names and he told me what he knew of them. There were many kinds of gums as well as stringybarks, mimosa and wattle. Cockatoos and galahs perched in their branches like pink and white flowers, their tuneless cries echoing along the track.

'Isn't it a fine day?' I cried out in delight.

'Indeed,' he replied, 'but any day that I have the sky open above me in a fine day to me.'

We plodded on. Storm clouds were beginning to gather and he wanted to make camp before the rains began. He chose a spot away from the main track and tethered the beasts nearby.

I watched as he lit a fire and hung a tin pot of water over it to boil.

'Can you cook?'

I nodded. He reached into a bag and brought out some bacon rashers and eggs.

I bent to my task while he made a damper from flour and water.

After supper, as the rain began to fall, I made to retire to the makeshift tent of blankets he had erected under a tree.

'I'll take first watch,' he said. 'I'll waken you in four hours.'

I had always thought that night was a silent time, but as I crouched over the sputtering fire clutching the rifle to me, I listened to a constant chorus of hoots and howls, barks and calls. The rain drizzled steadily and I was soon soaked through despite the heavy coat he had given me. My relief at hearing him stir just as the first light of dawn was edging above the horizon was immense. I added dry wood to the fire and set the billy on to boil.

'Good lass,' he said quietly.

I had never thought to hear anyone call me that again.

It took us many days to reach our first stop, the gold diggings at Bendigo. Occasionally we met some diggers on their way to Melbourne to spend their gold. They did not wish to linger so, after some tea and an exchange of news, they continued on their way.

Despite the discomforts of the journey, I found myself enjoying it. There were so many new sights and experiences that I only rarely felt the tedium. Kangaroos leapt out of our way, only to halt a few yards distant to turn and look quizzically back at us. Emus paused briefly in their foraging to regard us while all sorts of strange little creatures rustled away into the undergrowth as we passed.

Of where we were going, and of the land he owned, he would talk unreservedly. But at any mention of England, of the past, his brow would furrow and his lips remain firmly closed. I would have liked some reassurance on why he had been transported. I knew that many men had been sent here for very minor crimes or even for political agitation and I hoped that he was one of them. I could live with that. Yet I feared to ask too much about the past, not only because of his anger but in case he began to turn to me and ask the same. I would not know what to say. If I told him, what would he think of me?

I received that reassurance in an unusual way. While I was setting up camp after a good day's march, he went into the bush to look for firewood. When he returned, he reached into his pocket and brought out a handful of wriggling white grubs which he threw into the frying pan. I recoiled in horror.

'That's good food,' he said. 'Black fellas call them witchetty. Just because you ain't seen anything like it afore doesn't mean it isn't good. You got to look at things differently here. You can't keep your English values now. You got to look at things straight – ask yourself what you see.'

He lowered his voice. 'Like when I saw you at the pier. I saw a fine strong lass, fit to work aside me and help me. I didn't see nothing else about being a lady or that because it didn't matter to me. What matters is what you are now.'

I hung my head. I felt his great paw of a hand closing round mine and squeezing it briefly. Then he turned to the fire and poked it briskly.

At last we reached the diggings. It was an amazing sight. Coming out of the forest we were suddenly confronted by a vast plain of cleared land. Everywhere the earth had been disturbed and men's heads popped up from their holes in the ground like rabbits. The noise of digging, cradling and washing the soil was constant. Tents of all descriptions were set up around the workings, the larger belonging to traders who waited like vultures to relieve the diggers of their little bags of gold.

We camped a little way from the diggings and lit a fire. I mixed a damper and put it on the ashes to cook.

'Are you going to dig too?' I asked.

'No, I've done my stint. Got enough out to buy the land in South Australia. You got to know when to stop before the gold fever gets you.'

'What happens then?'

'Yon diggers we met on their way to Melbourne. That's gold fever. Dig, dig, dig till they strike it lucky, then off to Melbourne to spend the lot. A few weeks later, back they come to start all over again. And they're the lucky ones. Many of them don't strike gold at all.'

'Were you lucky then?'

'Yes and no,' he answered slowly. 'I dug a bit but found nothing but a few ounces. So I took to washing the gold from the soil. It's slow work but steady. The gold's there all right but it takes time to puddle it out. Most men ain't got the patience for it. Still, it made me enough money. Not a fortune, just enough to set me up.'

He stirred the fire.

'It's white gold I'm after now.'

'White gold?'

'Wool,' he answered. 'Wool's the coming thing. That's where the money lies. The land in South Australia is right for sheep and the market's demanding more and more wool so that's what we'll go in for.'

I saw more evidence of gold fever the next day. The load of provisions and stores we had brought up from Melbourne on the dray sold quickly at extortionate prices to the diggers. Even the bullocks and cart went. In the end, we were left with only sufficient stores to complete our journey and a tidy sum of money.

'Enough to buy some pretty good sheep,' he said as we loaded our bundles on to the mule and set out to walk the rest of the way.

It was a journey that should have taken us little more than a week. We set off early each morning, as quiet as we could so that he could shoot our supper on the way. Our fare was varied. One day he shot a goanna which made a tasty meal. On a bad day we made do with galah, a tough bird which needed a lot of cooking, whereas a kangaroo provided enough meat for several days.

We were nearing the township of Hamilton when it happened. He was clearing a site for the tent when he suddenly shouted for me. I came running to find him slashing at his leg with a knife.

'What are you doing?' I cried.

'Snake bite. Didn't see the damned thing. Suck for God's sake, suck the wound.'

I knelt over him and tried to draw the poison from his leg. I bathed and dressed it for him and helped him to a comfortable spot.

That night, fever overtook him. His brow was like fire and he raved and ranted in his delirium. I wrung out cloths in water and laid them on his forehead. I sponged his body and the scars on his back seemed to stand out like rope.

'Dear God,' I thought as I tended him, 'what must he have suffered.'

Towards morning, he quietened but it was not a restful sleep he drifted into. Instead his pulse weakened and his breathing became shallower.

'God, don't let him die,' I prayed. 'Let him live. I need him.'

His lips moved. I bent closer to him.

'Miriam,' he breathed. 'Miriam.'

I wept silently. I knew not who Miriam was, I did not want to ask.

All that day, I nursed him. At times, I thought he had gone, his breathing was so light. In the evening he passed into a deep sleep I feared would be his last. However, my prayers were answered for just as dawn was breaking, his eyes opened and he stared at me.

'Good lass,' he mouthed. 'Good lass.'

It was nearly a week before his strength returned and we could resume our journey. Our stores were greatly depleted by the time we reached Hamilton. It was good to be among people again. For the first time since leaving Melbourne I slept in a bed.

There were almost 50 families already in the area and more were expected in the months ahead.

'Where do the settlers come from?' I asked.

'Now lass, you should know better than to ask that. What does it matter where they came from or what they were? If they can't survive out here, then they're no good to man nor beast.'

We reached his property one evening as the light was going. We stood and gazed at the land covered in gum trees and stringybark, empty of any signs of civilisation but full of wildlife and promise.

'Tis good rich soil this,' he said, bending down and lifting a handful. 'It will carry a good head of sheep.'

He turned to me. 'God grant I can make a good life for us. It will be hard work for many a year ahead but with you to help me, we'll reach our goal.'

I gazed into his blue, blue eyes and smiled.

'Yes,' I said. 'We'll get there. Together.'

He bent and gently kissed my lips.

I was half a world away and I was home.

Knitting for Joyce

I'm knitting a cardigan for Joyce in a heather mixture double knitting wool and number 7 needles. It's quick to do and I'm already on the first sleeve and nearly up to the armhole. I've done the back and the left and right fronts and I only started it a couple of weeks ago. I showed her the pattern, buttons up the front to the neck and a collar, and she said she liked the style so I bought the wool and got started. I wanted it to be a Christmas present for her but she said to do no such thing and at least to let her give me the cost of the wool. The present could be the time I've spent on it. But you know, when you think of all she does for me, it's the least she deserves, so maybe I'll knit her a scarf and a hat to match as a surprise.

I look at the clock above the dresser again and then I get up and go ben the room to check on the one there on the mantelpiece. Yes, the one in the kitchen is right, it definitely is well past eleven and there's still no sign of her. It's not like Joyce to be this late in the morning to come in. She's usually here before ten to clean out the grate and get the fire going in here. It's cold and I shiver as I go over to the window and look out. Not that there's anything to see, the smog is that thick and you can't tell if it's day or night, it's that dark. Sounds are all muffled up like scarves round your neck. I hear a tram-car going down the street and it sounds like its wheels are covered in cotton wool, not rattly and screeching, as it rounds the corner. There's scarce anybody about, save a man, all wrapped up with his head down, disappearing into the gloom.

Everybody's staying put today. There's no point in going out when you can't see your hand in front of you. Even in the room it seems like there's wisps of the fog drifting by, seeping in through the window frames and down the chimney.

It's quiet and I can hear the clock tick, ticking away. The fire lies dead and the ashes are needing scraped out. Joyce usually does it for me and fills the coal scuttle as my knees aren't up to bending down to the hearth. I manage the kitchen range fine as it's not low down and the bunker is right there but I can't manage the room fire and I like it lit by eleven so's I can go in there and sit in an afternoon. What's the point of having a room and kitchen if you don't use the room? I like to sit in there of an evening and listen to the radio while I knit. I like the Scottish dance music with Jimmy Shand at half past six on the Scottish Home Service and after that there's maybe a play or a variety show so that before I know it, it's time to put my needles away and go ben the kitchen and get ready for my bed. It's always warm in there in the box bed as I keep the range going all night so's I can have my cup of tea in the morning.

But Joyce hasn't been in yet and I start to wonder what's happened. Maybe she didn't get home from her work last night if the smog was bad. She works in a pub in Argyle Street and usually doesn't get back till after eleven by the time they've cleared up. I can't see the attraction of sitting in a pub till ten o'clock at night though Joyce says they get quite a few women in the lounge bar. It wasn't the done thing in my day to go anywhere near a public house but things are changing that fast now. Joyce says they're going to get a juke box put into the lounge bar so's you can put money in and pick a gramophone record to play. Another thing apart from the beer to waste your money on.

I straighten one of my antimacassars on the back of the armchair. I mind when I sewed it for my bottom drawer and it looks all right despite being past forty years old. Though Joyce says they're out of fashion now but then what does an old buddy like me care whether I'm in fashion or not? I go back ben the kitchen and take up my knitting again. Maybe Joyce has had to stay the night with a friend if the buses aren't running. But the trams aren't off, they can always run in the smog as they can just keep to the rails.

I measure the knitting against the inch chart on the edge of the pattern. Another two rows should do it and then I'll start taking in for the armhole. It's just plain knitting, no fancy stitches or cables as I think you don't see the heather effect of the wool properly if you've got all those fancy bits and all. So I just purl away to myself for the next couple of rows.

It's been that good having Joyce across the landing. She moved in about a year ago and we've been friends since, even though she's in her twenties. She's that helpful and a good laugh. I mind when she came in to do my hair with one of the new home perms. What a time we had. It was a Sunday and we talked the whole time she was putting in the curlers and rinsing my hair. A friend had done hers the week before and I fair admired it so Joyce said she would do mine for me. I'd made some scones for when we had to sit and wait for the lotion to take. When Joyce had finished she held up the mirror so's I could see myself and then she bobbed down so's she was next to me and said, 'Which twin has the Toni?' We laughed till the tears were running down our faces. There I was, with all my wrinkles and her with her rosy cheeks and bonnie blue eyes and looking nothing like twins. What a laugh it was.

I look up at the clock again and it's getting later. She's maybe having a long lie though it's not like her, she's always up and busy. She's even started knitting. I couldn't believe her when she said she couldn't knit. What did they teach you at your school? I says. Did all wee lassies not get taught how to knit? But she said she was all butterfingers and the teacher always belted her for dropping the stitches and so she never learned. I rummled about in my knitting bag and gave her some left over green double knitting and a pair of size 8's. I keep my needles all together in another bag, all tied up in twos with a wee bit of the wool I last used them to knit something with. The size 8's had been a jumper for my nephew in a dark brown which I think he likes. It's never off his back anyhow.

Anyway, I casted on twenty stitches for Joyce and did the first row, just plain, to get her started. Then I showed her; in, over, through and off, in, over, through and off, but she was right about the butterfingers, more ham-fisted like. I never saw a lassie so awkward with her needles but she said she wanted to learn and did I not have any finer needles? I told her to stick with the big ones though they were that plastic stuff and not my good Aero steel needles. I didn't want to lose any of them but I didn't tell her that, I didn't want to hurt her feelings when she's that nice to me.

I can't settle to my knitting so I have a rummle in my bag and that's when I spot that one of my number 13's must have slipped out of its wool as there's only the one there. It's a right fine needle that 13, and I use them for shawls for the weans. Then I get that sore feeling in my heart even though it's near forty years ago. I'd knitted a bonny white shawl for him, all scalloped edges and fan-shells and I wrapped it round him so he was all cuddled up and put him in his wee box which was all we had to bury him in. 'That's a right waste,' my man said, 'burying him in a brand new shawl scarce used', but I knew I wouldn't be needing it again and anyway I wanted him to know

34

his mammy cared for him and I wanted him to be warm though I knew he wouldn't be warm ever again.

I feel a tear beginning to creep into my eye so I get up and pull the kettle over the fire and I take out a cup and saucer and the tin with my pancakes that I made for Joyce yesterday. She wasn't feeling herself and didn't have one. I wonder if she's all right – she's not been herself lately, a bit peely-wally and with no appetite to speak of. The pancakes are a wee bit hard now, they're always better fresh but I put them back in the tin because I'm wondering if maybe Joyce is not well and in her bed. The more I think about it, the more I realise that she's not been that great for a wee while. Kind of pale and down and … distracted.

I'm standing there wondering what to do when I see her key hanging on the dresser. I made her give me it after she was locked out once and had to get a man to break the lock for her. So I said I'd keep a spare key if she didn't mind and it's just as well as she's had to borrow it more than once. I'm wondering if I should give her door a wee chap just to check she's ok. I'm not wanting to be nosy like but it's gone twelve now and she's not been in.

I take the key off its hook and open my door. The smog's got in to the close and it's swirling about like wraiths on the landing. It's quiet, not a sound, and I hear my feet shuffle over to her door. I give it a wee chap and then another but there's no answer. I pause before I put the key in the lock, I don't want her to think I'm spying on her or anything like that but I'm worried. I open the door a keek and call 'Joyce' but she doesn't reply. I call again and push the door a wee bit wider and that's when I think she must have bought new linoleum as it's not the usual green, it's darker. But then something makes me go in and I see that it's not new linoleum, it's the floor that's wet and

35

sticky with dark stuff. My heart starts thumping and I push open her kitchen door and she's lying there on the floor and there's towels and sheets all about her and they're all stained, stained deep dark red and her face is that white and her rosy cheeks are all gone and her eyes, her bonnie blue eyes are closed and I know she's dead.

'Joyce,' I hear myself saying but I know it's no use, 'Joyce.' I realise what's happened, what she's done, poor lassie. I never even guessed she might be expecting and that's when I see it lying there on the floor in among all the blood, but still sharp and fine. My number 13 Aero knitting needle.

Bramble Jelly

Jeanette is making bramble jelly. She is trying to listen to the Morning Story on Radio 4 while she goes about her task. Jeanette's brow is furrowed as she weighs the deep purple fruit and tips the berries into the heavy jelly pan that belonged to her mother and is now dented and scarred with use, and her teeth bite her bottom lip. Carefully, she chops up two green apples, coring and slicing them and adding them to the pan with precise and efficient movements though her temples throb slightly. The radio continues a moving tale of survival, several sentences of which are missed as a lorry thunders by Jeanette's front door. She strains to hear.

Into a glass measuring jug, she runs cold water, holding it so that the meniscus is level with her eye. When she is satisfied as to amount, she adds it to the pan and turns on the gas. She picks at the dark red stain under her nails and waits for the fruit to warm. The rich sweet smell of the brambles fills her kitchen, lingering on surfaces and curtains so that the scent will still be there long after the jam is made. Several cars drive by and again the radio is drowned out.

Jeanette is making another lot of her prize winning bramble jelly and she fears it could be her last. Jeanette is famed among the local WRIs for her bramble jelly and she has won prizes for it at shows in the area. Sometimes she is coerced into giving a talk about making jelly and about brambles but she does not like public speaking and never gives away her recipe entirely. Heavily made up ladies with red nails and wearing wide brimmed hats strain to hear her quiet voice as she speaks of the uses of brambles in times past. Of how Nicholas Culpeper, in his Complete Herbal of 1653, recommended bramble leaves boiled in lye for the treatment of itch and sores of the head and for dyeing the hair black. Of how, even today, bramble leaves are an effective remedy for diarrhoea and for sore throats and mouth ulcers.

Jeannette lowers the gas to simmer as the brambles heat and fall apart in the ruby liquid. She will let it cook until the fruit is soft and then she will mash it to a pulp of shimmering rubescence.

Jeanette also knows much of the folklore surrounding brambles. 'Sitting under a bramble bush was supposed to cure rheumatism, boils and blackheads, while the arch formed by a rooting shoot was regarded as magical and children were passed through it to protect them from various disorders,' she will say to her audience. Apart from the ladies in hats, there are usually several farmers' wives, recognisable from their thrown together outfits, ruddy cheeks and lingering smell of the milking parlour. Neither group will ever make bramble jelly, the ladies because of the scrambling and scratching among the plants necessary to pick the fruit and the farmers' wives because of their chronic shortage of time. But they like to hear her speak of the processes involved and after, sample her jelly on home-made scones.

But this could be the last autumn that she gathers the fruit. She has her own special patch, the situation of which she has divulged to nobody. She found it many years ago when she was newly wed and went for long, time-consuming walks away from the house. Her husband came with her once, just the once, shortly before he disappeared. He did not like picking brambles though he always ladled the jam generously on to his toast.

She had to persuade him to help her that time, leading him on through the dense undergrowth to her patch.

Over the years, the brambles and nettles have grown thicker and denser, twining and intertwining into an almost impenetrable mass. Since her husband left, she has come alone every year to pick the fruit and to tend what she considers to be her own piece of ground. It is deep in a stretch of woodland, near to the river but far enough away from the main paths. It is a struggle to get through to it, but Jeanette has gradually trodden a narrow way through.

At the height of the brief brambling season in September, Jeanette can pick three or more pounds in an hour. She holds her bowl under the fruit and the ripe ones simply fall into it. Towards the end of September, the fruits are smaller and then she will also pick some red ones to provide the pectin the jelly needs, instead of using the green apples. But she always leaves enough berries to ripen and seed and fall to the ground and grow new plants and she spreads out the long branches and pins them down into the earth to root. In this way, the bramble patch has grown from what was, those many years ago, a relatively small patch, into what it is today, covering the entire banking and spreading across the original paths.

'I never pick the fruit after September 29th, Michaelmas,' she says in her talks. 'It was believed that after that date, the devil spat and urinated on the berries.'

Another huge lorry rattles past shaking her windows. Certainly, the new bypass will leave her house and those in the rest of the village, in peace. She and her neighbours will be able to walk safely along the road, will be able to reverse their cars out without fear of being hit, will be able to hear the punch lines of jokes in the comedy shows on TV. Yes, the bypass will bring many benefits to Jeanette and her neighbours. But the bypass is going straight through her bramble patch.

Jeanette sets a large bowl on her kitchen counter just under the shelving. She has a system whereby she can suspend her jelly bag from a wooden spoon inserted in the handles of her cupboard doors. She ladles the dark plum-coloured pulp into the jelly bag and the first of the blood red juice drips through into the bowl. She will let it sit there all night until every last drop is drained.

'Brambles will grow anywhere,' Jeanette will tell her audience, 'in many different kinds of soil but they benefit from some feeding, a bit of blood and bone suits them fine.' Over the years, she has almost become an expert on rubus fruticosus, the wild bramble. 'They grow in all kinds of soil and in full sun or shade. They do like a moist soil, hence they grow well here…' A slight murmur of laughter.

Jeanette does not sleep well that night, her tossing and turning punctuated by the occasional traffic sounds and by the steady drip of the crimson juice. For picking the berries, she wears an old jacket her husband once bought her and which she has never liked. Although it has been washed many times, it still carries a reddish brown tinge which will not fade. Her hands tingle from the numerous nettle stings she receives as she plunges her hands into the deepest niches where the best black clumps are to be found. She does not mind the pain of the stings and scratches, she is used to them and feels that they are only what is due to her.

The bypass worries her. There are public meetings but Jeanette does not stand up to speak out against it. Instead, she murmurs in the ears of the made up ladies and to the farmers' wives as they pull on battered coats before rushing off to the next milking. The ladies talk amongst themselves, shaking their heads over the disturbance of it all and of course over Jeanette, shame she never remarried. She was quite young when he left suddenly. Nobody had ever heard from him again. Australia, some thought he'd gone to, or was it New Zealand? Looked such a happy couple too but you never can tell what goes on in a marriage.

Jeanette can. She never missed him, though she played the part of the deserted wife well. She felt such relief after he was gone that she sometimes had to remind herself to look down-hearted and sad. But she never felt tempted to repeat the experience.

Jeanette has spoken to many people about her fears for the woodland. She presses small jars of jelly, taken from her cupboards where they lie like necklaces of garnets, into the hands of councillors, planners, her MP, her MSP, even her MEP. She talks quietly and they nod their heads and take her jam and are reminded of her as they spread it on their toast and scones.

The next morning after breakfast, Jeanette carefully removes the bowl full of ruby red juice. 'Never squeeze the jelly bag,' she always tells her audience. 'That way the jelly becomes cloudy.' When she first made bramble jelly she would pound the mush in the jelly bag with a heavy meat tenderiser her husband gave her the first Christmas they were married. But now she knows better and the meat tenderiser lies unused in a kitchen drawer, still stained and dark from the juice of the berries of long ago. She has scrubbed it often, but the stains never totally fade.

She measures the liquid in her jug and pours it into the pan. Sugar is weighed and added and the pan left to come to a rolling boil. She warms the sterile jars in the oven ready for the hot jam. A saucer sits in the fridge, cooling, to test for setting point. This is the crucial part. Nothing must go wrong or Jeanette be distracted. She watches the jam froth and bubble, pink and purple, its sweetness filling the air and her mouth salivates.

The phone rings. But Jeanette cannot answer it. The jam cannot be left. She might miss the setting point and all will be lost. The answer phone switches on but a convoy of trucks rumble by and she cannot hear the speaker. Never mind. When she is finished, she will deal with it.

She tests a little of the jam on the cold saucer but it is not yet ready. Patiently she waits, testing every few minutes until at last, a skin wrinkles under her spoon. Quickly she switches off the gas and brings out her jars. The pink scum is removed and the jam stirred. She pours the hot red juice into the jars, filling them almost to the top. When the last spoonful is emptied from the pan, she tops each jar with a wax disc and sets them aside to cool. She likes the look of them. It appears to be a good making, this one, this last one perhaps.

Jeanette washes her hands of the stickiness and goes to the phone. It is one of her farmers' wives. The voice is excited as well it might be. The council are buying their land for the bypass. It will not now go through the woodland and the bramble patch. It is to be preserved as a site of environmental importance due to its untouched nature. The council will ensure it stays that way.

Jeanette stretches the cellophane circles over the jars and fastens them with an elastic band. Carefully she writes out the labels. Bramble jelly and the date. A last rub and then she lines the jars up in the cupboard along with the rest. They glow like beads of arterial blood. She switches on the radio to some music. Classic FM is playing the Waltz of the Flowers. She hums along and is happy.

Jeanette's bramble patch will remain undisturbed. And so will the quiet tenor of her life. Let her husband rest there in his shallow, unmarked grave. Blood and bone give nutrients to her brambles. For once, he'd done some good.

A Man's a Man for a' that

Surely the most appropriate person to invite to the Alloway and Ayr Robert Burns Poetry Festival was Robert Burns himself.

It was my duty and pleasure to invite him. I have studied his works for many years and devoted my life to the reading of his poetry. He has been my hero (what an overused word to describe my obsession with him and his work) and the opportunity to meet him would be the highlight of my whole life. Nothing was too much for me as far as he was concerned. In fact, I was prepared to die for him.

It took a bit of arranging. Time of my death, whether temporary or permanent, manner of death, where exactly he was, were all matters I discussed with the agent. Despite some trouble with the seventh commandment, the adultery one, he had in fact been accepted above and not consigned to that other place.

The date was set for my demise. I concentrated hard on what my first words to the bard should be. It was while I was turning over such weighty questions that I stepped out in front of the number 77 Express bus to Glasgow.

Despite knowing that this was the day, a surge of anger at the incompetence of drivers rose in me and I managed a weak shake of my fist at the underside of the bus before I succumbed.

I must confess to being keen to see the pearly gates and St Peter with his open ledger, so I was extremely disappointed to find myself outside what looked like the entrance to an NCP car park. A metal pole blocked my way and in a small porter's lodge sat someone with his face hidden behind a copy of a newspaper (it was the Glasgow Herald appropriately enough) and his feet on the table.

I tapped sharply on the window.

'Yes?'

'Are you St Peter?'

'No, I'm St Leger. It's St Peter's day off. What do you want?'

I showed him my special pass and he consulted a scruffy piece of paper decorated with coffee rings.

'Right, you can go in.'

He pressed a button and the barrier rose.

I walked into Heaven. I was enraptured. Now, where would I find my hero?

An angel was hovering nearby, picking his nose I was horrified to note, so I tapped him brusquely on the wing.

'Can you tell me where I can find Robert Burns?'

'Which one? Robert Burns, plumber and heating engineer, Robert Burns, the dearly beloved infant son of Margaret, Robert Burns, one time teacher of English, Sir Robert Burns,...'

'...the poet,' I interrupted. 'Scotland's Bard.'

'Aw him,' replied the angel. 'Follow the mists until you find him. He's aye staring at his feet and muttering.' And why not, I thought? Of course he would be still writing his immortal poetry.

Then I saw him. He was sitting on a grassy knoll, with his chin resting on his fist and his eyes gazing ahead. A perfect sight, a vision of our greatest poet at work. I stood quietly, not daring to interrupt his reverie.

This was the moment I had been waiting for. This was my destiny. There he was, Robert Burns, the Bard of Scotland, still communing with his Muse.

I stood there in silence. Unfortunately, my stomach gurgled noisily.

'Got a wee touch o' wind in the baggie?' were his first immortal words.

'Mr. – er – Burns,' I stammered, my face reddening with embarrassment at the thought of what deathless prose my previous night's chicken vindaloo had spoiled, 'I've been granted a short visit to speak with you.'

'Are you frae Hell?' His face brightened visibly. 'Any chance o' getting me a transfer oot o' here?'

I was transfixed.

'Why would you want to go there?'

'Bit o' life, ye ken.'

I thought at first he winked, but it must have been a trick of the light.

'Unless of course, you fancy a bit of houghmagandie yersel?'

I recognised the old Scots word though its precise meaning escaped me for a moment. But the wink this time was unmistakable, accompanied as it was by a nudge in the ribs. I understood. He was going to sing to me.

'I'd love that,' I enthused. 'Do you want me to join in? Or would you rather I just sat back and let you perform by yourself?'

'Just do what you feel like, hen,' he said. 'I'm no that fussy after all this time.'

He took my hand.

'You'd better watch him,' a cherub said cheekily as he passed by, hitching up his cloud. 'He's only got one thing on his mind.'

Of course he had. How else could he produce such phrasing, such sentiments, such beautiful lyrics if his mind was not constantly in the act of creation?

'Mr. Burns,' I began again, 'or may I call you Rabbie?'

'Why?'

'Well, everybody else does. Rabbie Burns. You're well-known.'

The swear word exploded from him. An Anglo-Saxon one that I was shocked to hear coming from him.

'Who tellt on me then? Was it that bitch o' … naw, naw, it was her wi' the big…' His hands described two round objects. 'It was, wasn't it?'

I looked at him blankly. He drew himself up to his full height, which was less than I'd expected from his portrait, and peered up into my face.

'Who was it?'

'Nobody,' I tried to reassure him. 'I only meant that you're well known because of your poetry. You're famous.'

'Ma poetry? Are you still reading it?'

'Oh yes,' I sighed, and bursting into song, I gave him the opening lines of his loveliest.

O, my luve is like a red, red rose that's newly sprung in June…

He didn't seem to like it and muttered something about eldritch skriechs.

'What else do you ken?'

'Tam o' Shanter, The Cotter's Saturday Night, Address to a Haggis, To a Mouse, Scots Wha Hae, Ca' the Yowes, Auld Lang Syne, Ae Fond Kiss…' I paused for breath. 'John

47

Anderson, my Jo, Holy Wullie's Prayer, To a Mountain daisy, To a Louse…'

Burns' draw dropped.

'You mean, it's lasted aw this time? Aw these wee bits o' scribbling? Ah cannae believe it.'

'Yes, your poems are known throughout the world and *Auld Lang Syne* is sung everywhere and there are Burns' Suppers held world-wide on your birthday and not only that, I'm here to invite you to the Alloway and Ayr Robert Burns Poetry Festival.'

His eyes lit up and he laughed.

'Aye there'll be a fair wheen o' Burns in Ayr by noo, are there no?' He nudged me in the ribs again.

I paused. 'Yes there's…. and …' I mentioned two of Ayr's worthies. 'But I don't know if they're descended from your line.'

'They probably are. I did my bit to help the population roon aboot.' And he winked again.

That was just like Burns. To be so generous in helping out those less well off than himself. Man's humanity to man, to paraphrase his own immortal words.

'Ah'm looking forward to seeing the auld toon again,' he continued. 'There's nothing to do up here aw day long. Mind you…' He looked me up and down. '… you'd do at a pinch. Ye cannae be fussy aboot an old raincoat on a wet night.'

I pondered over the deeper significance of his utterings and was unaware of his arm moving around my waist until suddenly, he pulled me towards him and planted a slobby kiss on my lips.

'Fair fa' your honest, sonsie face,' he began.

I tried to push him away but though he was small, he was strong – and desperate. His hands wrestled with my Marks and Sparks pure wool skirt and tangled with my underwear.

'Mr. Burns!' I shrieked. 'Remember who you are!'

He obviously did for he redoubled his efforts and pushed me to the heavenly ground.

I tried to remember what the lady self-defence expert had suggested when she spoke at the Ayrshire Ladies Lunch Club and attempted to knee him but unfortunately missed.

His hands were definitely where they shouldn't have been.

'This won't hurt,' he was saying. 'This won't hurt.'

'No, no,' I murmured as my strength failed, while part of me kept whispering, 'A man's a man for a' that...'

'No,' I said more loudly. 'You are hurting me.'

A jolt of pain shot through me and I opened my eyes. I found I was staring at the underside of the number 77 Express bus to Glasgow.

'This won't hurt,' a voice repeated and I looked into the face of an ambulance man who was gently moving me on to a stretcher.

'You had a lucky escape,' he said.

I nodded. I certainly had.

However, notwithstanding his unfortunate..er... behaviour, may I present to you, Mr Robert Burns.

Secrets

Sometimes secrets should remain so for ever.

I stir my coffee, add a touch of milk and a spoonful of soft brown sugar and wait. I need Anya.

She bustles in, her blue uniform crisp as always, her eyes heavily mascara-ed. Too much, I keep telling her, but she ignores me and plasters it on regardless.

'You want a leetle something?' she grins, her accent even more pronounced than usual. 'Our leetle secret.'

I nod. She pulls open the door of my wardrobe and delves into the dark recesses behind a suitcase. I don't know why I keep my suitcase. My only way out of here will be in a box, or in one of those over-grown wicker hampers which my daughter favours as being ecologically sound.

'Believe me, death is no picnic so why should I go out in a hamper?' I say to her.

'Mum,' she laughs. 'Still as sharp as ever.'

Anya produces my bottle of Laphroaig, half-empty now, and opening it, pours a hefty slug into my coffee. She knows how I like it.

Our leetle secret. That and the tumbler I have at bedtime. On her days off, I suffer. I don't see why I can't be open about it but if I wish to continue my sojourn here, then I must eschew alcohol.

My coffee after lunch sets me up for the afternoon visit of Patricia, my daughter, she of the giant-sized picnic hamper. Patricia goes to a genealogy class on Thursdays and is at present researching my side of the family. She is happy and interested and I intend that she stays that way.

For a long time, she was not happy. After her dad died, she grieved deeply. So did I but it was tempered with relief that at least that was one person less I could hurt. Patricia adored John and he was devoted to her, his only child. They were so happy in each other's company that I knew I'd done right by keeping quiet. Why hurt those you love in the name of truth?

I sip my coffee and taste the whisky as it eases its way down my throat. Anya has been generous with her helping, as well she might, seeing that I'm paying for it twice over.

I give her money to buy more when the bottle is running low and she short changes me every time. She thinks I don't know, that my eyesight and memory are failing.

'That was a ten and a twenty you gave me,' she says, handing me a few coins in change. I know it was two twenties but I keep quiet as I want my whisky and if I argue, she might stop buying it. So I keep my secret to myself.

Just as I drain the last dregs, Patricia arrives with her family tree. After the usual pleasantries, she unrolls it and spreads it across my table. She points firmly at Grace, from two generations back and a cousin several times removed. I have no recollection of her at all.

'You weren't quite right about her,' she says, her finger jabbing at the name. 'She didn't have an illegitimate daughter, not that I could find, but she was pregnant when she married.'

I nod. I feed her scraps of imaginary information to keep her focused on my side of the family. The more skeletons she can find, the happier she is.

Rather these ones than those that rattle in other cupboards.

I'm good at keeping secrets. That's how I got the job at the doctor's surgery. I did his filing and answered the telephone and

51

when he was out on his rounds, read the notes on patients and squirrelled away interesting little snippets. Not the right thing to do or a nice thing, but maybe I'm not that nice a person. No doubt I'll receive my just desserts when I'm carted off in my wicker hamper.

That's how I found out about John's problems. It was in his files. I knew he'd had a difficult childhood, in foster homes, never knowing his real family. And just as well, as apparently, he suffered from congenital syphilis, passed on to him in the womb by his mother. His eyes had caused him problems but there was another side-effect; the possibility of his being infertile. We'd never had children even although we'd been married for several years by then.

He'd never mentioned it so I suspected he didn't know himself. In those days, information like that wasn't divulged to patients. All John knew was that he had a bit of a problem with his eyes.

'I'm going to look at Grace's son's family next,' Patricia says. 'If I can find a wedding or death certificate I can trace his descendants. Maybe I'll find some long-lost cousins somewhere.'

I smile at her. Patricia has always felt the lack of a large family. She has two children of her own, my grandchildren whom I adore unconditionally, but I think if they could have afforded it, she and Matthew would have had several more. Don't push your luck, I had wanted to tell Patricia. Don't push your luck.

She prattles on happily and quizzes me about various other far-flung family members long dead and only vaguely remembered by me.

'He was a right character, that one,' I lie. 'I think he was some sort of commercial traveller.'

Poor great-uncle Percy was probably a pillar of the church and never put a foot wrong in his life. Patricia circles him on the family tree as a potential subject worth investigating.

I want her to keep it to my side of the family. I don't want her investigating John's.

'You like some tea, Mrs Maxwell?' Anya pops her head round the door. 'Milk, no sugar, I remember. And you Jess?' She pronounces my name as if it has a z at the end – Jezz, as if it's short for Jezebel.

I nod and smile at her as she shuts the door.

In bed that night I think back to when I worked in the surgery. The doctor was, I suppose, quite an attractive man with those startling light blue eyes and a Cary Grant dimple on his chin. John had thought it a good idea for me to work as it would stop me brooding on my lack of children.

He felt he'd been proved right when after a year or so, I became pregnant. I was horrified and guilty as I'd been having an affair with the doctor. Actually, 'affair' aggrandises it far too much; it was only several quick couplings in the cupboard after the patients had gone. But the guilt was awful. How could I do that to John? I suppose I found it exciting in its way.

The doctor offered to terminate it for me if I wished. But I didn't. This was my only chance to have a child and I wasn't going to destroy it.

'I just hope for your sake it doesn't have a dimpled chin,' he said.

In the event, Patricia was the double of me even down to my hazel eyes and thin fine hair. She was a delightful child, all smiles and dimples, fortunately not on her chin.

I had given up my job in the surgery when I became pregnant and had little to do with the doctor afterwards. The local midwife attended Patricia's birth and she was a healthy child so it came as shock to learn that the doctor had died. A shock, but also a relief. Cancer, it was whispered with much pursing of lips. Not even the doctor could beat that dread disease.

The next day is one of Anya's days off so I'm not in the best of moods when Patricia visits. She's not toting the family tree this time. Instead, she's worrying about James, my grandson. He's had kidney problems since birth and has been in and out of hospital many times.

'We were wondering if there could be a genetic element,' she says and my heart starts to beat erratically. She goes on about various tests available while I feel myself becoming light-headed and dizzy. Eventually it is even apparent to her.

Before I know it, the nurses are bundling me into bed. The charge nurse gives me some medicine which knocks me out for a while.

When I wake, Patricia's at my bedside with Matthew, her husband.

'I'm still here,' I mumble. 'Cancel the wicker hamper.'

'Mum!' she laughs. 'Really!'

They leave me to recover in peace. I think back to the first time John and I met Matthew. One Christmas, Patricia told us there was someone she'd like us to meet, one of her college lecturers. John and I were thrilled at the thought that this could be her future husband.

I almost passed out when she brought him to the house. The pale blue eyes and dimpled chin were only too distinctive. He was the image of his father.

Matthew Maxwell. I didn't know what to do for the best. John of course was delighted at the prospect of the match. I could only shiver inside.

I urged Patricia to be sure she was making the right decision until she asked me outright if I didn't like Matthew. I had to say that he was a lovely young man, and he was, and back off.

I remember every moment of their wedding service. When the minister intoned if anybody has any objections, speak now or forever hold your peace, the silence seemed to hang over me like a shroud. It was as if the ghost of Dr Maxwell was hovering. The pause felt endless. But I kept silent.

For my sins, I suffered over the next few years as they first produced a daughter and then a son. When James was found to have kidney problems, I blamed myself. I should never have allowed the wedding to go ahead. But no mention was made of hereditary possibilities. Until now.

I'm still not myself the next day and when Patricia comes, I feel like sending her away but instead I try to listen as she relates the news from home. I feel my eyes closing until a phrase catches my attention.

I rouse myself. 'What did you say?' I ask.

'Matthew's dad,' she says. 'If only they'd thought to test his dad rather than his mum they might have discovered the cancer earlier.'

'Test what?'

'Mum, you haven't been listening. One of the first signs of testicular cancer is infertility. Matthew's parents were trying for another child but had no luck so Matthew's mum went for testing to see what was wrong. If only they'd tested his dad, he might still be here.'

'He was infertile?'

'Possibly. But in those days they assumed the woman was at fault, especially as she'd had two children already.'

I have a sleepless night as I digest this information. By the time Patricia was two years old, Dr Maxwell had died. So what were the chances that he was already infertile when we'd had our affair?

And what were the chances that John wasn't totally infertile? And that working in the surgery (and having the affair) were enough to trigger my hormones into life, enabling me to conceive?

I won't ever know the answer to all that. And I'll leave it to further generations to find out. Some day maybe my grandson or my great-grandchild, if I have one, will take up where Patricia leaves off and investigate the family tree. Maybe DNA testing will be only too common by then.

The next day, there is a lightness in my heart. Perhaps now I can forgive myself my sins.

When Anya brings me my coffee after lunch, I resolve not to mention the little matter of money to her. Some sins should be over-looked. Others should be allowed to die with those who know them. And buried with them, more likely in an over-sized wicker hamper.

Ped Xing

The first time it happened, I was standing at a crosswalk down town. It unsettled me though I put it down to overwork.

I guess we all wonder what our worlds would have been like if we'd taken the other road. Six years ago, I'd reached a watershed in my life, and I'd made a decision then which, though it seemed out of character to my family and friends, I've never regretted.

I came out here to South West Florida to work. I chose Fort Myers simply because there had been a jumbo-sized postcard pinned up on the kitchen wall of the flat Steven and I had shared in Glasgow. It was a picture of a long strip of beach fringed with palms and the sun going down in a purple-rose sky. Across it were slashed the words 'Hi there from Fort Myers!'

I gave up my job and my live-in lover and came. At first I clerked in a real estate office but soon I realised that there were plenty of business opportunities going. The snowbirds (senior citizens from the North who come down to Florida to winter November through April) needed someone on hand to check out their condominiums and trailer homes during the summer months when they returned north. As well, I took on renting the condos to summer visitors and my business really sparked. I had my condo on the beach where after work, I could sit on the veranda sipping iced tea and watching the sun setting in a purple-rose sky.

So it came as quite a shock that day while I was waiting at a crosswalk (or ped xing as the signs all call it here) to realise that I was crossing at traffic lights in Glasgow and not only that, pushing a double buggy as well. The wheels caught on the far kerb and I had to lean the pram back before I could get it on the sidewalk. But when I did, I found I was back in Fort Myers.

I tried to put it out of my mind as a one off, and anyway, I was far too busy to waste time on it.

When it happened again, it shook me. Several weeks had gone by and I was heading into a downtown shopping mall to buy something to wear that evening on a date. I pushed the heavy doors at the entrance and found myself in Marks and Spencers. I was pushing the double buggy and heading for the children's section. I saw myself browsing through the baby clothes, looking at girls' aged six to twelve months. One of the babies in the buggy began to grizzle so I made my choice, and, making motherly soothing noises, headed out of the store.

I was back in Fort Myers, standing outside the mall holding a Sears dress bag. Inside, sure enough, was a dress. I drove home, pretty shaky this time, and tried it on. It fitted me and I liked it. But I had no recollection of buying it. While I had bodily been in Sears buying dresses, I had also managed to be in Marks and Spencers several thousand miles away. What gave me the shivers most of all was that at no time had I felt uncomfortable or unreal or fearful of the situation. On the contrary, I had felt quite at home.

I mentioned my experience to some friends.

'You're working too hard,' one had said. 'You sure look tuckered out. You need a holiday.'

But I was too busy then for that.

It happened more often. It seemed to occur most when I was crossing an intersection. One moment, I'd be watching the

DON'T WALK sign and the next, there would be the little green man and the shrill beep beep beep and I'd be back in Glasgow. I began to call it my ped xing feeling which was after all, quite appropriate. I was making a crossing of a kind, of miles, of minds, of lives.

One night, I woke suddenly. I'd been in a deep sleep but something dragged me from it into a half waking state. I clambered out of bed and staggered into the next room. I saw myself pick up a crying baby and pat and soothe it to sleep again. I seemed to know what to do and where everything was. I put the baby back in her cot, checked on the toddler in the other bed and tiptoed back to my room. There was a large bulky figure at one side of the bed. I knew this was Steven though I could not make out his features. Snuggling into his warm back I fell asleep. When I awoke, it was to the sun streaming through the blinds of my condo on the beach.

I tried a holiday. I went to friends in San Francisco but it seemed I spent most of the time sheltering from the rain on the Isle of Arran. I decided to talk to my friends.

'Have you noticed anything strange about me this holiday?' I tentatively asked Elmira.

'Strange, honey?' she said. 'Why?'

'Well, different, not quite here.'

'No I can't say that I do. I thought you looked a little peaky when you arrived but that's all gone. You look real relaxed now.'

'You haven't felt I've been well, absent?'

'Absent? No honey, you're all there.' She laughed. 'You've got to be with a business like yours. How could you be such a success otherwise?'

So obviously there were no outward signs of my ped xings. Logically though, it bothered me. If I was here in Florida, how could I possibly be back in Glasgow too? It was as if there was another me, leading a life parallel to mine except that that she had taken the other road six years ago when I decided to leave. I had felt my life narrowing, had seen what lay ahead if I stayed. It wasn't that it would be so awful to stay and marry Steven but in my parents, I saw us thirty years on. Steven hadn't seemed to understand.

'We can go abroad on holiday if you want,' he'd said.

'It's not that I don't love you,' I'd said and stopped. 'I want to see a bit of the world before we settle down, find out who I really am.'

Steven had laughed. 'You'd be hopeless on your own. You couldn't cope. I wouldn't be around to pick up all the bits every time you fell to pieces. What about your job? We need your tiny earnings to help with the mortgage. You can't give that up.'

But I did. And Steven too. Even on the way to the airport he was still suggesting that I was being stupid, that I wouldn't manage, that I could turn back right now and carry on as before.

This other me had turned back and had stayed in Glasgow, married Steven and had two children. They were still living in the flat that I had shared with him.

I went to my doctor. She examined me carefully and pronounced me physically fit although my cholesterol was slightly high.

'And I suggest you take more exercise,' she continued. 'It will help you cope with your stress levels.'

'But what should I do?' I asked desperately.

'I can give you the name of a good psychotherapist if you like.'

I shook my head and left.

The ped xings continued. The depth to which I was becoming involved with my other half's life intensified. I found myself actually worrying about the baby's lack of weight gain in the middle of a call to a client in Michigan.

A letter from my mother gave me an idea. Why should I not find out what had happened to Steven? That way I would know if what I was experiencing in any way resembled real life.

My mother's reply was brief. Unable to take in the fact that I had wanted to leave Scotland, she had decided that Steven must have driven me to it and since then, contact between them had ceased.

'I believe Steven is married,' she wrote, 'though who to I have no idea. Apparently they have two young children and are still living in the flat you had.'

So was I going mad or was I living a double life? How could I logically be in two places at once, living two completely different lives? But apparently I was. The ped xings were increasing in frequency and length. Almost half my life was back in Glasgow, going to the library, the baby clinic, the supermarket – a mundane existence that had me gritting my teeth in despair. So did my alter ego. I felt her despondency and depression as day after day, she tried to cope with the children, the draughty flat, the dreariness of her life. I felt her thoughts turn eventually to suicide and watched as she toyed with the packet of paracetamol and the bottle of Valium in the childproof bathroom cabinet. She was at the end of her tether and so was I.

On one occasion when I was aware that I was back in Florida, I decided to help her out and hopefully at the same time put an end to my ped xings. In the glove compartment of my car, I carried a small ladies' pistol which I bought after some guy had tried to assault me one night on my way home.

61

He had pulled open the car door when I was stopped at a red and grabbed me. Luckily there was a couple in the car behind who yelled at him and he ran. But ever since, I'd carried the gun just in case.

Now I took it out of the compartment and slipped it into the pocket of my jacket. From then on, whatever I was wearing I made sure the gun was on my person. I wasn't sure if I could take it when I crossed over but I could try. So I waited for my next ped xing. It came soon enough. I found myself in the kitchen of the flat trying to light the gas oven. It had always been difficult to light, the gas pressure not being as strong two floors up. I had apparently been making scones and the lumps of dough sat on trays ready to bake. I decided to make a casserole for tea and chopped up the grisly meat into cubes. I prepared the vegetables slowly and carefully as the knife was sharp. When I finished I put the dish into the oven along with the scones. I was feeling less despairing, I could sense, in fact there was an aura of anticipation, of eagerness I couldn't quite fathom.

I made a cup of instant coffee and sat down at the same old table with the red plastic top cracked at the corners.

The outside door banged and the curtains trembled in the draught. Steven came into the kitchen, shedding his wet anorak.

'Something smells good,' he said, kissing my hair. 'You're looking better. I must say, it's nice having you back to normal after all this time. You weren't yourself at all.'

He went over to the kettle and switched it on. His back was to me. The excitement in me was rising. I could feel the icy sweat trickle down my back and the rapid pounding of my heart.

I stood up and reached into the pocket of my jeans. I didn't even aim before I pulled the trigger. The noise was stunning and my wrist hurt from the recoil. Steven staggered against the wall, arms akimbo, and slid to the floor. As he did so, he knocked off the jumbo-sized postcard of the beach and palm trees at sunset with 'Hi there from Fort Myers!' across it.

In the next room, a baby started to cry.

The Darkness Before Dawn

Across the silent city, Sabeen hears the faint call to prayer of the muezzin. It is time. Dressed in the dark clothes of her dead brother, she slings her bag across her shoulder, turns to look at her parents sleeping side by side on the rough floor, and sets out.

It is the hour before dawn. The earth is stilled, at the height of the pendulum swing, pausing before beginning its descent into a new day. A light wind stirs the vestiges of the night.

Sabeen steps quietly across the threshold of what was once their home and slips along the well-trodden path through the rubble. She stays close to the walls, slipping unseen through the darkness. Her steps are measured, careful to feel for solid ground, silent so as not to reveal her position. Not even a shadow betrays her movements. Across the wide, empty street she makes out the ruins of other shops and houses. There stood the spice shop once owned by old Ahmed with the one eye. Sabeen can almost smell again the rich aromas of cinnamon and turmeric, nutmeg and paprika in the air. Further on, the halal butcher's where her mother, dressed in her black burka, purchased their lamb and mutton, goat and occasionally beef. Where once her friend Lilith's parents had their fabric stall, a riot of colours and patterns, a single piece of tattered blue silk flutters. The shops are all gone now, nothing remains but desolation.

She wonders if Lilith has made it safely out of the country. They left almost as soon as the fighting started, bundling up their most precious belongings and filling their battered old car with them. They were heading for the border but she has not heard anything of them since. Lilith said she hoped they might end up in America; she would prefer that, she said, to one of the neighbouring countries. But Lilith was always a dreamer, always wanting what she could not have.

Sabeen knows nothing of their fate. No news. Nothing. But they at least, have had a chance to escape. Maybe they are safe, maybe they are in a refugee camp, though she has heard terrible tales of what happens in them. Maybe, maybe.

She slips behind a pillar as she hears a truck backfire its way along the street. Whether it is a government vehicle or one of the radical factions, she does not know. Nor does it matter. They are all the same, those rough, bearded men toting Kalashnikovs. After the first rape, she cut her hair short. Jagged, haphazard slashes with scissors. Her father wouldn't look at her, refused to ask her why, knowing yet refusing to acknowledge it. Her mother retreated further into her own world, shutting out all her torment, unable to cope with what was happening around her.

The truck shudders off towards the centre of the city to whatever place they plan to search, to destroy. She peeks from her hiding place and spots a figure across the street, silently stumbling through the rubble. Friend or foe? Man or woman, she cannot make out. More likely someone like herself, out looking for food, for aid, for anything to provide some comfort. But she cannot be sure so she waits till they have passed on. The air is chill at this time and Sabeen shivers despite the layers of clothing. At first it had felt strange to be dressed in male clothes but now she feels it makes her stronger, that the spirit of her brother is with her, helping her find her way through this new, ugly world.

Sabeen steps out again. Under some fallen masonry she spots a remnant of cloth. Carefully she extracts it. It is filthy, tattered but usable as a curtain perhaps to shield her family from the cold winds or as an extra cover for her mother lying on the ground. She folds it as best she can and tucks it away in her bag before moving on.

Dawn hints that it is not far away. There is a lightening in the sky so she hurries on, aware that she must return before daylight makes her presence more visible to others. She moves past what was her father's car showroom, once light and attractive and brilliant with new, polished, latest model cars. He would not leave his business. He did not want to flee and let others plunder his life's work. So they stayed while Lilith and her parents left their stall unprotected and fled. Now there is no difference between them. Both businesses are gone long since, but whereas Lilith may be safe, Sabeen and what remains of her family are quartered in the downstairs kitchen of their home surrounded by bomb debris and haunting memories.

She feels that something is behind her, following her. No sound but goose bumps flow down her arm. Is there or isn't there someone there? She daren't breathe, listening to her heart hammer in her head, listening for a sound to betray another's presence. Not again, please. Not again. Seconds pass in an eternity of time. Then a faint miaow and she lets out a long sigh. The cat she found as a kitten in the rubble desperately nursing from its dead mother has followed her. She waits until she feels it rub against her leg and bends to stroke its soft fur.

Scary cat, she thinks as it purrs and rubs her hand. Together they make their way further along the street, she ignoring the glimpses of what the buildings once were. There is no point in looking back, in wishing for happier times. What is gone is gone. Best to concentrate on surviving another day. Maybe one day, when there is peace, when life is normal again.... But Sabeen knows that the old order is gone for good. What lies ahead no-one knows.

The cat's eyes gleam gold in the dark. She follows it, ducking under slabs of concrete, scrambling over broken doors and distorted window frames. They both turn away from a smell she has come to recognise. Death is never pleasant. The cat leads her to what has been a home almost as spacious as her parents' once was. The door to the street has been blown away and the roof has collapsed but most of the walls defining the rooms are still standing. She wanders through what might have been the women's quarters, secluded from the street, her eyes peeled for anything that she can use. She picks up a piece of coloured glass and wonders what it came from. A lamp? An ornament? Her feet crunch on other glass shards and she stumbles as a sharp splinter threatens to pierce her sandal. Whose home was this? And where are they now? In her memory, she walks the street as it once was trying to picture the inhabitants and to place the house in her mind's eye but it escapes her. Even the geography of her city has changed, blown apart by the bombs and the fighting.

Sabeen cannot, must not linger, she must make her way back before daybreak. She has no food yet so she tries to head towards where she feels the kitchen must have been. There would be a cool pantry too, where foods would be kept from spoiling. But there is nothing. Cupboards lie empty, their doors swinging drunkenly on their remaining hinges. Anything that was there has long been looted. She turns to go. The cat is sniffing at a small door in a corner that lies slightly ajar. She bends down to look and sees something shiny. A can. A can of something edible perhaps. The label is soaked with rain and water from the burst pipes and almost indistinguishable but it could be food. Reaching in, she finds another and another though some have burst open and their rancid contents spill over the floor. She stuffs the undamaged cans in her bag until it is full and she can carry no more. Tonight they will eat. Tonight they will sleep with full bellies. Perhaps her mother will smile again. Perhaps her father will be able to look her in the eye. Perhaps.

She begins to head out of the building. Somewhere she takes a wrong turn and finds herself in the inner courtyard. In the centre stand the remains of a fountain, dry now, its spouts streaked with a green algae. The pond surrounding it contains some brackish water, its former level marked by a stain of dark green, in which a tiny dun-coloured bird slakes its thirst. She pauses but the bird senses her nearness and flies off in a flutter of feathers and a warning chirrup. At the far side of the courtyard, a tree struggles to survive. Only a few yellowing leaves are left on its lower branches. Some of the upper branches are blackened like teeth. Not so long ago it would have provided shade for the house's inhabitants in the heat of the day, a place of comfort and coolness for the women to sit.

A glimpse of something lighter in shade catches her eye. On a straggly bush near the fountain a flower has opened. A pale gleam marks it out. She creeps along the walls of the courtyard until she reaches it and steps out towards it. It is a rose. A pale yellow and pink rose almost fully opened. She cups it in her hand and bends to smell its fragrance. After the foul odours which have dominated her days, it seems ethereal, from a different, almost forgotten world. For a moment, her surroundings disappear and she is transported into an alternative life, a life she once had. Today the sun will bring the rose to its full flower and despite there being no-one to appreciate its beauty, it will continue its cycle and set seed for the future.

Unseen above her on a neighbouring rooftop, a sniper picks up his AK47 and clicks off the safety catch. He is watching, waiting for something, someone, anyone. He has seen Sabeen.

Sabeen is still savouring the rose, touching its velvet petals with her thumb, when she hears the cat miaow again. Her reverie is disturbed. Wildly, she glances around her, and, bending her head, scurries for the shelter of the walls. She darts into the darkness, her breath uneven, and waits till she calms, till she feels it is safe to move again. The cat rubs against her ankles. Silently, they begin the journey back. As she reaches home, the sky bursts into pale pink and yellow washes across the city.

The sniper rests his weapon on the ground beside him, lights a cigarette and resumes his vigil.

A new day has begun.

Some Things Never Change

Jimmy peered through the tiny porthole window as the plane lumbered down through the clouds. That at least hadn't changed. Clouds. Masses of great grey dirty ones full of rain. Then like the switching on of a light, green fields, hills, water.

He could see Arran with its grey cloud crown but now its fields were dotted with white whirling wind turbines. Power for the people, Jimmy thought. He looked across to the other side of the plane hoping for a glimpse of the Ayrshire coast, haunt of his childhood summers, but the opposite window was too far away beyond the rows of people for him to see.

'We are now approaching Glasgow West International Airport,' the disembodied voice said. 'Please do not leave your seat until the plane has been fumigated and energy passports checked.'

Jimmy patted his top pocket. It was nestled in there, beside his ticket, a small green document printed on recycled paper, an anonymous piece of writing for which Jimmy had strived for nearly fourteen years. His own personal green passport. He had eschewed meat for the entire time, living off pulses and soya protein, fruit and vegetables from his plot, home made flat bread baked in the communal oven, eggs from his chooks and the occasional find of dead kangaroo. But it had all been worth while. Here he was, within a stone's throw of landing on his native soil, of returning home. To Glasgow. A dragonfly shiver flashed through him as he watched the land, his land, approach and envelop the plane in its welcome.

The Australian news media had carried tales of life in Scotland when home news was pushed to fill the daily, hour long slot, and letters from friends had arrived after the long sea voyage, their cramped writing filling every available scrap of paper, so he knew of the hardships faced when the oil and gas ran out. But it was the same everywhere. Resources worldwide had been squandered and nowhere was life as easy as it had been, though Jimmy had to admit that Australia was one of the better places to live, not having heating problems and bills to contend with. And if it did get too hot, then a dip in the ocean was cooling and health positive.

The plane turned to make its final approach. Jimmy glimpsed crowds of people lining the runway fences, watching as the 800 seater plane nosed its way carefully down to land. Only one flight a month was allowed to Glasgow, and Jimmy had had his name down for a flight for many years. His careful recycling of household goods, clothing, waste and non-use of power apart from that afforded by his own self had earned him extra green points towards the coveted passport. And now here he was, about to touch down on his native soil. He was home.

The red tape surrounding the landing of such a plane and so many passengers was tedious and time-consuming but eventually Jimmy followed the trail out into a dreich drizzle of a Scottish March morning. He shivered while simultaneously exulting in the soft rain on his face as he plodded across the road for the train to Glasgow Central. Boyhood pleasure filled him as he saw it hissing and steaming at the platform. Steam. They were using coal again.

He lifted his black plastic bag of clothing and other essentials, his Glasgow suitcase, on to the train and found a place for it on the luggage rack. He was lucky that like many Glaswegians of his generation he was small and slight so that

71

his weight allowance had been relatively generous. Anyone over 200 pounds was forbidden a luggage allowance and those unfortunates weighing more than 250 pounds were forbidden to fly at all.

The train puffed its way across Ayrshire and up to the outskirts of the city. Even here, the countryside refused to give way and fields of winter turnips and kale were planted right up to the foot of the high rise flats so that they rose out of a sea of purple green. Gardens were being prepared for spring plantings and compost bins bulging with rotting organic waste guarded the perimeters.

The train slowed as it crossed the Clyde and gave a half-hearted whistle. Below in the water, Jimmy watched a man row a wooden boat laden with bundles of old newspapers upriver while several small sailing boats tacked to catch the morning breeze down to the open sea and the fishing grounds. Other rowboats were kept busy carrying foot passengers from one side of the river to the other, darting between the larger multi-sailed boats laden with Ayrshire coal or luxury items like tea and coffee.

The Kingston Bridge was packed with cyclists crossing into town and whatever work they could find, while one of the flyovers, Jimmy noticed, had a flock of sheep grazing along it as if it were the slopes of a ben. Like all sheep, they ignored the flurry of life beneath them.

Central Station was much quieter than he remembered. The crowd from the train quickly dispersed and Jimmy stood in the empty concourse, alone save for a few wily pigeons that had escaped being shot for the pot. Even his breathing seemed to echo among the roof girders. He hefted his black bag on to his back and walked slowly down the stairs to Renfield Street.

Jimmy's eye took in the boarded up shops, the street empty of traffic but full of people searching for any useful rubbish that might have been dropped. Several men and women bundled in kenspeckle and well-patched clothing shouted their wares. It took Jimmy a few minutes to tune back into the accent.

'Paa-perrr,' shouted one. Jimmy felt in his pocket for a few coins. A newspaper was a luxury but he wanted to know about Glasgow now, about the muggings and the gossip and the ads and what films were showing, if any. He wanted to be part of the city that had been the vibrant womb of his youth.

'How many?' asked the vendor.

'Just the one.'

'Three pun.'

Jimmy handed over the cash, mentally adjusting his budget. Who could buy papers if they were that price? FLOOD FEARS INCREASE screeched the headline. WATER RESTRICTIONS TIGHTEN.

The drizzle dampened the page as he read. The rest of the page was taken up with shortages of goods, the forecast of cuts in power usage and a report on the increasing debts as a result of the Olympic Games in London. Confused, Jimmy read the masthead. 17th August 2013, it said. Almost ten years ago. He'd paid three quid for a newspaper that was ten years old. He carefully folded it and walked back to the vendor.

He waited while a woman counted out some coins for a single sheet.

'It's out of date,' Jimmy said.

'They all are,' said the man. 'Whit date were ye wantin? Ah've got 2006, that's wan fifty, or a 2020 for twenny quid.'

'What about today's?'

The man snorted. 'No such thing, son. If ye want the day's news, read it oan the parliament windaes or wait fur the crier tae come roon. Ye'll catch him in George Square at noon.'

Jimmy slipped the paper inside his jacket. He'd read it later. Old news was better than no news and it would pass the evening if his lodgings ran to candles, that is.

He wandered into Buchanan Street searching for something that remained of his past. What, he didn't know, but he'd recognise it when he saw it. That flare of identity would flash over him and he would feel, really feel, that he was home again.

He mooched along, pulling up the collar of his jacket against the rain. A beggar sat in a doorway sheltering from the persistent drizzle, his grey hand outstretched.

'Got onythin spare?' he asked. Jimmy gave him the recycled plastic cup he'd taken on to the plane with him so that he could buy a drink of water on the long flight. The beggar grinned and slipped it inside his jacket.

'Thanks pal,' he said. 'Like gold dust these are, gold dust.'

Jimmy nodded and walked towards George Square. This was where he had once worked as an assistant to one of the councillors. His office had overlooked the red asphalt with its statues planted like calcified trees and from there, he had watched the citizens going about their business. Now there wasn't time to sit and watch others, not if you wanted to eat.

The smell reached him first, a smell he recognised as that of the farmyard. Before he arrived at the street corner, Jimmy knew what would be there. He was right. The Square was divided up into small allotments and each section was tended by a small army of men and women and the occasional child, digging and breaking up the soil for summer crops. A cart laden with manure was selling it by the shovelful and the reeking odoriferous material was being laid over the earth with a reverence due more to a Wee Free burial.

Jimmy walked along the side of the Square towards the City Chambers. He wanted again to look up at the window of the office where he had worked, for old times sake. His eyes counted the rows of great sash windows. Three along and two down on the right. There it was. Dark, boarded up like all the rest. Empty of councillors and their minions. He waited for the flash, for the shiver, for any emotion, but none came. He stood in the rain and felt only damp and chilled.

He stepped off the pavement to cross the road. Suddenly he was jerked backwards as a great grey shape whished silently passed him. A bus. A huge number 45 of an electric bus, Jimmy noticed while conscious of a tugging at his back. He turned round to see a wee woman clutching the tail of his jacket.

'Nearly got yer troosers pressed fur free there, son,' she said. 'You got to be careful o these big lumps o transport. No like the auld yins. At least you could hear them comin, when they did.'

'Yes, thanks. I wasn't paying attention. I was looking up at the windows. I used to work there years ago.'

'In there? Wi the cooncillors? See ma sister's man, he had a fell oot wi wan o these cooncillors on account o' his bad knees an' at. No the wan wi the three hooses, the other wee scunner, the wan who'd pit the boot in the taxi scam. Ye mind o the taxi scams?'

Jimmy nodded, not that he did, but he didn't want to interrupt the flow of the old woman's tale.

'Well, ma sister's man, no Magrit ma ither sister, Betty .....'

And on she went, her whole life story spilling out as Jimmy stood there listening to her broad accent and feeling the smirr of rain settling on his head and shoulders. Jimmy leant against the bus stop and stuck his hands in his pockets to keep warm.

He let the cadences of her voice wash over him leaving a slow warmth to creep through his bones to his soul.

Some things never change. Nothing had really changed. No matter what happened to Glasgow, there would always be a wee wifie telling her tale to a stranger at a bus stop. He was home again.

Peach Melba

Lucy pushed her wheelchair to the table and looked at the three faces gazing at her.

'I'm Lucy,' she said.

'So am I,' said the lady to her left, 'and so is Margaret but Betty comes and goes.'

'Jean's a bit deaf,' said Margaret. 'She doesn't hear what you say.' She turned to Jean and raised her voice. 'This is Lucy and she's lucid too.'

'Pleased to meet you,' said Jean. Margaret smiled and Betty grinned.

A carer who looked about sixteen came in with their meal. 'Here you are then, ladies, your favourite, Margaret, mince and carrots and mashed potatoes!'

Margaret squealed. 'Oh thank you, Kelly, you're so kind.'

Lucy stared at the watery mince and grey potato. Nothing like what she used to make.

'Bloody pish,' she said under her breath.

Betty laughed and winked at her. 'The food's what you'd call plain and mushy for the benefit of those with no teeth. No cordon ....' Her eyes glazed and she stared at Lucy.

'She's away again,' said Margaret. 'Sometimes she's with you most of the day and sometimes she drifts away quite a lot. Senile detention.'

'What?' asked Jean.

Margaret raised her voice again. 'Detention! Senile detention! What Betty's got.'

'That's exactly right,' said Lucy. 'And we've all got it. That's what this is, senile detention. My son came home when I took badly, stuck me in here and now he's buggered off back to America.'

She shoved her fork into the mince and mixed it into the potato. It turned a deeper grey. 'You bring them up as best you can and then they can't wait to get rid of you. Selfish pig!'

'It's beef actually,' said Jean. 'Pork mince is not so nice. Too fatty for my liking. It leaves a scum on top of the gravy.'

'I don't care what kind of mince it is, it's still pish.'

'Don't get too excited,' said Jean in a loud sotto voce. 'Margaret's heart, you know.'

Margaret nodded, her face flushed. 'My heart can't stand too much excitement, it's not good for me. The doctor said I was not to get excited.'

'Well you're not likely to get excited here.' The only sounds that Lucy could hear were the faint rumble of traffic beyond the double glazed windows and the click of Jean's false teeth as she worked her way steadily through her meal.

'Where are the other residents?' Lucy asked.

'They either eat in their rooms if they're bedridden or they get fed in the other lounge,' explained Margaret, nodding over to the door.

'They're gaga in there,' said Betty. 'Somebody shoot me before it's my turn.'

'You stay with us then,' said Jean. 'Stop wandering off in wee dwams.'

Lucy felt a dark shadow drift near. The home had looked so fresh and well appointed, more like a hotel, that she'd almost looked forward to leaving the hospital and moving in. God's waiting room, she thought, before realising she'd said it aloud.

'And the owners run the funeral parlour next door,' said Betty. 'So convenient, don't you think? It makes me want to die of some contagious disease that will contaminate their sluices.'

'Oh Betty,' said Jean. 'Stop that, you're putting me off my food.'

Lucy played with her mince and finally put down her fork and knife.

'Who's got a nice clean plate?' The staff nurse bustled in. 'Well done, Margaret darling.' She reached over and hugged her.

'Is it peach melba for pudding?' Margaret asked.

'Not today dear, but we've got yummy semolina.'

'I love peach melba,' said Margaret. 'I used to have it when my husband took me out for a meal. We went to the Clarendon hotel on a Saturday night and I always had peach melba. It had tinned half peaches in it and loads of raspberry sauce.'

The staff nurse tutted at Lucy's plate. 'We didn't do too well, did we?'

'It's not up to my own standard,' said Lucy.

'It takes a wee while to settle in, just give it a week or two and your appetite will pick up.'

'Not for that stuff,' replied Lucy, ducking as the nurse tried to hug her. 'Perhaps you should start giving out gold stars for clean plates. That might encourage us to eat up.'

The sarcasm was lost on the nurse.

'Now that would be a good idea. Clever you, Lucy.' She hugged Lucy before she could dodge and carried off their plates in triumph.

'Is she a lesbian?' said Lucy.

'No, I think she's from Glasgow,' replied Jean.

Lucy found the days long and the food bland. Breakfast at eight, tea at eleven, lunch at one followed by a nap then tea at four and high tea at six and bed at eight. On Sundays a variety of ministers took it in turn to visit and on Tuesdays it was the hairdresser, Wednesdays the chiropodist and Fridays bingo. Lucy missed her battered old armchair which fitted her body and comforted her aches. She missed her window which looked on to the school playground and the street and she missed her smelly old cat who crept under her blankets at night and had been her only companion in the years before her stroke. She knew she could not go back to her flat, that she could not look after herself any more, but she would have given anything to live there again. Only the company of her dining companions lightened her humdrum existence in the home.

One day about three weeks after her arrival, when the food had been particularly mundane and the nurse very touchy-feely, Lucy said, 'I'd love a decent meal in civilised circumstances.'

'In a hotel,' said Betty.

'With polite and discreet waiters,' added Jean.

'And peach melba for dessert,' said Margaret.

'Well why don't we?' said Lucy.

The others looked at her.

'How?' they chorused.

'What's to stop us?' said Lucy. 'We can come and go as we please, surely?'

'The door's locked,' said Margaret. 'So that Betty can't wander off.'

'The code's beside the door,' Betty said. '7353. Just press the buttons and we're out.'

'What?' said Jean. 'I can't hear.'

'Shh!' said Betty. 'We don't want the staff to know.'

'We can phone and book a table for lunch and get a taxi there and back,' said Lucy. 'You cause a distraction, Betty, and I'll phone from the office.'

Half an hour later, a loud wailing came from the lounge and as staff rushed towards it, Jean wheeled Lucy into the office. Before Betty had finished her drama queen act, the hotel and taxi were booked for a late lunch the next day.

They had planned everything to avoid suspicion. The nursing home chips and macaroni lunch was quickly stuffed into a plastic bag and disposed of in a bin and four clean plates were left for the staff nurse.

'Well done, girls,' she said. 'Another gold star for you all.' Lucy endured the hug for the sake of their outing.

Then, as the other old dears and the staff settled down for their rests and coffee, Betty punched the code in and quietly opened the front door. Jean wheeled Lucy down the ramp and Margaret followed clutching her handbag.

'Come on Betty!' she urged. 'Keep with us!' For a moment, they stood there, waiting for a voice, a figure to appear, their break-out to be foiled, but nothing happened. A sense of freedom like a caterpillar wriggled down their spines and galvanised them.

'Out into the street,' said Lucy. 'Catch the taxi before it turns in.'

It was a bit of a struggle getting Lucy in her chair up the ramp the driver provided but they all managed and the taxi moved away without being spotted.

As it pulled up in front of the four star hotel, Jean said, 'What about money?'

'Just send the account to the home,' said Margaret to the driver. 'My husband always charged things.'

It was as much a commotion getting them all out but a couple of young porters helped.

'In for your lunch, girls?' asked one.

'I hope you've got peach melba,' said Margaret. 'It won't be the same if you haven't.'

'Good afternoon ladies,' said the maitre de, ushering them into the dining room. 'Drinks?'

'Whisky,' said Lucy. 'Your best.'

'And wine with the meal,' said Margaret, whose face was flushed. 'I'll choose it.'

Betty's eyes were glazing again. 'Come on,' said Jean. 'Stay with us. You want to enjoy this.' With an effort she pulled herself into the present and smiled. 'Wonderful idea, Lucy.'

The meal was leisurely, civilised and the waiter didn't attempt to hug them once for leaving clean plates. The steak that Jean ordered was tender enough for her false teeth to tackle without too much clacking and Lucy tucked into her beef en croute ('Steak pie frenchified but bloody good') with relish.

And Margaret sighed with pleasure as the waiter brought in a huge peach melba, overflowing with cream and raspberry sauce and decorated with a parasol, fresh summer berries and a sprig of mint.

'This is heaven,' she said as she dug her spoon in and brought out a slice of peach. Even the fact that it was fresh and not tinned, didn't spoil it for her. 'Delicious,' she said. 'Like spring and flowers and... and being in love for the first time again.'

Jean and Betty and Lucy laughed but each knew that feeling and warmed themselves at its brief glow.

After, they sat in the lounge with their coffees and looked out over the hotel gardens.

'This is civilised,' said Lucy. 'Why can't we move here?'

Betty snorted. 'Do you think the government would pay for it?'

Margaret's face was red with wine and food. 'I haven't enjoyed myself so much since my husband died. This has been just superb. I'll always remember this day. Thank you for arranging it, Lucy.'

Jean was nodding off. Soon the others followed. The staff tiptoed past them. The afternoon drifted by with only a gentle snore to disturb it.

When Lucy woke, the shadows were beginning to fall across the garden and the maitre de was standing in front of her.

'Madam,' he said. 'Your friend ...'

'What?'

'Your friend....'

Lucy looked round. Jean's mouth hung slightly open and Betty stared straight ahead smiling at something only she could see. Margaret had slumped forward in her armchair until she was almost bent double.

'She can't be comfortable like that,' said Lucy. 'Can you move her back?'

'I think she is ill,' he said.

'No she's not, she's just sleeping. She always has a nap after lunch. She's got to take it easy because of her bad heart.'

'Yes madam,' he said. 'I will call an ambulance.'

'Jean!' Lucy shook her. 'Wake up!'

'What?'

'It's Margaret. She's not well.'

Jean's eyes slowly focused on her.

'Can you move her so she's more comfortable?'

Jean pulled herself out of the armchair and got hold of Margaret's hand. It was cold.

'She's not ill, she's dead. Her heart must have given out.'

Jean and Lucy sat on either side of Margaret holding a hand each, and waited, watching the shadows cover the garden and the colours fade. The day was almost over.

The ambulance came and took Margaret away from behind screens the porters erected to shield their other customers from her. The staff nurse and two assistants arrived in a fury to take their escapees back to the home.

'You killed her,' the nurse hissed at them. 'What am I going to tell the family?'

'You'll tell them she died a happy woman, in the company of friends and after a good meal out,' said Lucy. 'Which is a damn sight more than we'll get to do. Now take us back to the home.'

'It was all worth it,' stage whispered Jean as she climbed into the home's minibus. 'Margaret had the best day of her life in years. That's the way I want to go, if you can arrange it.'

Lucy smiled. 'I don't think so. We'll just have to live on our memories.'

Betty had retreated into hers.

Lucy watched the darkening streets slip by like passing years. Soon it would be night.

About the Author

Ann Burnett has written many short stories and been published in New Writing Scotland, the Woman's Weekly, My Weekly, That's Life (Australia) as well as M.Phil student anthologies published by Freight. She has also been a scriptwriter for BBC children's radio and TV programmes and writes online travel and general articles.